Morning Glory
Blossoms

Suchittthra Shreiyaa Lakshmi Vasu

Edited by Rajesh Kumar

PARTRIDGE

To order additional copies of this book, contact
Toll Free 800 101 2657 (Singapore)
Toll Free 1 800 81 7340 (Malaysia)
orders.singapore@partridgepublishing.com

www.partridgepublishing.com/singapore

Dedication

To my beloved parents, Krishna and Shantha Vasu; my family; the entire Vasu–Daver family, especially Aravind, Tanaaz, Zahaan, Dilly, Roxana, Peter, Maya, Cyrus, and Laila.

To my mother, especially, who was my first guru in writing. I am humbled with gratitude and give her thanks for recognizing my writing skills and giving me my very first lessons on how to write.

To my large circle of invaluable friends, especially my college mates from St Andrew's Junior College (1979): Nabs Naidu, Thaker Sabir Husain, Sundaram Subramaniam, and the whole lot.

Special thanks to Mathew Kurian, an eminent lawyer, who vetted the legal aspects of this book and gave his endorsement that this book is a pure piece of fiction from my imagination and is a creation of my mind, and Rajesh, editor in chief of *Pravasi Express* newspaper, who edited the book.

To all the people who came my way to give me love and support and to teach and guide me with good lessons in my life.

I am grateful to my divine masters for their spiritual guidance and blessings; my doctors, who made me well; my country for making it safe for me to live in as a single woman; my teachers and my lecturer when I was at Monash University (Melbourne), who guided me to write my master's thesis, which was published in Geneva. Thereon began my journey to write, which has been a fulfilling and gratifying one. I worship writing as it runs through my jugular vein and sustains and nourishes my soul.

All of you are special to me in a very deep way.

Most of all, thanks to God Almighty for giving me the gift of writing.

Chapter 1

Once upon a Time

Once upon a time, Kajal Shreiyaa had a life that anyone would envy. She came from a respectable home of means and had everything anyone could ask for. She was a happy, sprightly child with a host of dreams about love, light, and hope. This is a tale of Kajal Shreiyaa's life. She found love and had great expectations that did not materialize into reality. Dreams were broken in front of her, and she began life as a young woman shattered. The torrential rains pelted in her life, and the tent had caught fire. From what was a joyful childhood, her early adulthood was full of pain and anguish. Life became a struggle, but she weathered the storm with the support of her family.

Shreiyaa will tell you how it turned around. None of what happened in her life were her dreams; they were the by-product of a higher power. She realizes that nothing really is very much in our own hands and there is a higher power that dictates and is the architect of our destiny. And you cannot change the will of God. Her own dreams were shattered, yet another dream became a reality. Then it turned around again, and the sunshine peaked through but with a different sort of light. Destiny brought her to new places and to new people, and the unexpected happened in her life.

Kajal (which is black kohl, put on the eyes by ladies as a highlighter) is the dark side of Shreiyaa's life, and Shreiyaa (meaning auspicious, magnificent, and lucky) is the bright side of Kajal Shreiyaa's life. Altogether the journey of life has taken her to a different destination. And there are treasures at the end of the rainbow. Shreiyaa's life is a mix of pain and sorrow, excitement and adventure. And how her strong inner spirit makes her life beautiful again despite the odds is the journey of this book. She leaves the Kajal out of her life, the dark side, and strives to mend the broken pieces with Shreiyaa, reaching greater heights with a naturally endowed gift from God—the gift of writing.

The new destination she arrives at is in seeing her words take the print form and inspiring others with words that sing from the deepest and innermost core of her soul. This is an expression of love for her, and she has arrived at a new destination in the light, out of the dark tunnel of pain, sorrow, and depression. This new destination is a world stage for her to perform, and she loves every moment of it. The phase of Kajal is now out of her life, and Shreiyaa will tell you her tale on how she got to be magnificent and lucky again as a writer and author.

Shreiyaa's story is a story of success when she climbed out stinging from the hot, burning fires of the cauldron of a broken relationship and losing a loved one. She has today found a meaningful purpose in her life. The journey of Shreiyaa's life is recorded in this small book, which has a serious intent. It is done to help people in similar situations or to help those faced with other tragedies to travel on the road less travelled and recreate a new and resourceful destiny—a destiny that one can be proud of and a destiny that will earn one respect from others and a destiny where one will also respect oneself.

You can rebuild with faith in your creator if you are spiritual; if not, in yourself. But in doing so, you must have a strong conviction in your heart to embrace good values and principles in your life and in your dealings with others. It is the golden key to new and greener pastures and rich harvest ahead. When one door has shut behind you, you can open a new door or new doors ahead in your life, and you should make the best and most out of your life!

Kajal Shreiyaa's Parents before Her

Kishen Venugopal and Nandini Venugopal are her beloved parents, originally from North Malabar, Kerala, in South India. Now they are amongst the pioneer generations of Singaporeans.

Kishen was born in 1921 and Nandini in 1929. They are Malayali by origin and Hindu in faith. Malayalam, the native language of Malayalis, has its origin from the words *mala* (meaning 'mountain') and *alam* (meaning 'land' or 'locality'). Hence, the term Malayali refers to the people from the mountains who live beyond the western holy side of the river, and Malayalam is the language that is spoken there. They speak both Malayalam and English.

A Little about Their Roots: Chokli and Eranholi Thalassery

Her father, Kishen, was born in a village called Chokli in the Kannur District of Kerala in South India. He is of North Malabar origin. Chokli is a village in Thalassery Taluk (a subdivision of a district or a group of several villages organized for revenue purposes).

Chokli is 7 kilometres from Thalassery and 458 kilometres from the state capital, Thiruvananthapuram. Nearby is the Arabian Sea. The weather is either hot and humid or wet and cool in the monsoon season. Malayalam is the local language.

This part of Kerala is blessed with crystal-clear waters running through their lakes and rivers and abundant river fish. It also boasts of coconut trees that line the beaches, lakes, and river banks. Coconut is the land's most important fruit, known as the tree of a hundred uses. Coconut milk is used in curries and for medicinal products, coconut water from tender coconuts is a wonderful thirst quencher, the stem of the leaves is used to make brooms for sweeping, and tender coconut is used to make a delicious coconut liqueur called toddy, which tastes like the Caribbean Malibu.

North Malabar

North Malabar starts at Korapuzha in the south and tapers off at Manjeshwaram in the north of Kerala. It consists of the former royal principalities and fiefdoms of Kolathu Nadu, Kadatha Nadu, and southern part of Tulu Nadu.

Going back in time to the early medieval era, North Malabar preserved its distinct political identity. The Chera Dynasty did not control this area, and that is why even today the area boasts of a unique cultural identity.

When you compare the rest of Kerala with Thalassery both in its geographical and cultural make-up, it is distinct in many aspects of the word.

The indigenous people is comprised of Hindu natives, Muslims (locally known as Mappila), Jains, and migrant Christians. The Arabs, Chinese, and Jews were deeply involved in the spice trade during the yesteryears. Thalassery was a haven for growth and sale of peppercorns, and it was abundantly harvested and formed part of the spice trade.

The people of Thalassery are so proud of their unique and distinct culture and traditional values and their identity that up until the early twentieth century, it was rare for any intermarriage. They jealously guarded their blood and would not allow for outsiders to marry into their families. There were social taboos attached with other communities so that it was forbidden for their women to marry anyone from the southern territories.

Even today marrying someone in the southern territories is frowned upon, so much so that when they place newspaper advertisements for a marriage alliance, they would openly make known their preference that the prospective bride or groom should hail from North Malabar and not Travancore. If you are from North Malabar, you should only marry someone from North Malabar because that is the ideal choice for a life partner.

This is how they think in Thalassery. This trend of thought is the jugular vein that runs in the blood of all the people of North Malabar, and it is still preserved even today. Today you can see that the Malayalis live in bigger houses and each home is blessed with prosperity that came from them and went out of the country to Dubai and other Middle East countries. Locally they would say, 'Ar vedu Dubai kash', meaning that the house has Dubai money!

Malabar Women: A Must-Mention

Malabar women are by far some of the most beautiful women in the world. They are naturally endowed with well-toned, shapely bodies and are fair-complexioned even though they are thoroughbred South Indians. Why Shreiyaa says this is because North Indians have the advantage of mixed blood of Aryan descent, which give them a fair complexion. Malabar women do not have this, yet they have a beautiful complexion. They say they are of wheatish complexion, which is fair, with a hint of a golden highlights on their smooth-as-silk skin. They have neatly chiselled features with sharp pointed noses and eyes formed like a perfect lotus petal. Their eyes gleam with inner and outer radiance, and when they are clad in sari, it is indeed a joy to watch them with their charming feminine demeanour.

They are house-proud women who are sticklers for cleanliness, a quality which derived from their mostly Hindu background. Hinduism venerates the woman as the mother goddess. The mother goddess takes three forms: Durga, Mahalakshmi, and Saraswathi. Durga is worshipped for eradicating vices, Mahalakshmi as the goddess of wealth and abundance, and Saraswathi as the goddess of learning and knowledge. The Hindus predominantly propitiate the universal mother goddess and put her on the pedestal and worship her. Most women in Malabar try to emulate the mother goddess, aiming to assimilate all her divine qualities. So in essence, cleanliness is next to godliness, and therefore they keep themselves clean (so too their homes) to invite abundance into their lives.

The sari is the most graceful of apparel, and they will wear ornate gold jewellery and gold bangles with strings of pristine jasmine flowers in their hair. This they will do when they set out in the mornings to begin their day by worshipping in a temple. It is such a pretty sight to see these sari-clad women in an array of multicoloured floral and other patterns.

They also smell as fresh as flowers after having bathed in sandalwood shavings. Perfume is natural, and most of them do not use make-up. They are naturally beautiful to look at. To the Malabar woman, marriage is very significant. Their husbands take the role of head of household, and children are brought up with much care and love.

Shreiyaa's mother, Nandini Venugopal, is from Eranholi, Thalassery, North Malabar, also in Kerala. Thalassery has a culture of its own, and it is worth knowing about it, as much of it influenced her parents' lifestyle when they emigrated to Singapore. They jealously guarded their Indian values but were also open to mingling with the multicultural society of Singapore. Though their values were old-fashioned and steeped in tradition, you could say they were altogether ahead of their times.

Major Festivals in Kerala

Two major festivals in Kerala are Vishu and Onam.

Vishu is the New Year, whereas Onam is the celebration of the harvest festival. Vishu in Kerala is Puthuvarusham for the Tamil and Vaisakhi for the Punjabis. It all falls around the same time of the year and is usually celebrated with a sumptuous vegetarian spread known as a *sadhya*, which literally translates as a 'banquet'. Onam is mainly celebrated with a large vegetarian spread served on banana leaves. It is normal for households to make a carpet out of flowers. Called a *pukolam*, it is placed on a plank of wood, and a picture or motif is drawn then decorated with a lovely array of colourful fresh flowers. It is placed at the entrance of the home. The more artistic the person doing the pukolam, the more spectacular the result will be.

Thalassery Cuisine

Shreiyaa includes this because it is unique to her parents' origin and very delicious.

Thalassery is known for its biryani (in local dialect, *biriyaani*). Unlike other biryani cuisines Thalassery biryani uses *kaimal/jeerakasala* rice instead of the usual basmati rice. The Arabian/Mughal influence is evident in its culinary culture, especially in the dishes of the Muslim community, although many have become popular amongst all communities. Kerala, a state in the south-west of India, is known as the Land of Spices because it traded spices with Europe. Also, most of these spices were home-grown, especially pepper from Thalassery.

Food is served on a banana leaf, and almost every dish has coconut and spices added for flavour, giving its cuisine a spicy taste that tantalizes the palate. There is also a liberal use of tamarind to make the taste of the food piquant. Seafood is the main diet in coastal Kerala. Meat is served as the main course in tribal and northern Kerala. Dishes range from simple porridge, known as *kanyi*, to lavish feasts, or sadhyas. Coconuts grow in abundance in Kerala, and as such, coconut kernel (sliced or grated), coconut cream, and coconut milk are often used to thicken and flavour dishes.

Now let Shreiyaa tell you about their awesome mouth-watering Thalassery biryani, which is the signature dish of the Malayalis from Thalassery. Shreiyaa also wants to add that this dish is cooked to perfection and served in copper bowls. Not too greasy and incredibly delicious, Thalassery biryani is a hybrid of *dum* biryani but has an originality and culinary individuality of its own. It is sometimes called green biryani because the masala is different from dum biryani, which uses saffron liberally to make it look orange in colour. The concept is similar. Either fish, prawn, chicken, goat, or mutton is cooked with rice, but in this case, the mixture of masala is a combination of mint and coriander.

Another name for this biryani is also Malabar biryani, a very popular choice for wedding banquets in Malabar, Kerala. It is traditionally served on banana leaves, and the accompaniments are mint chutney with a touch of desiccated coconut to give it full body, achar (or mango or lime pickle), and raita, a refreshing cold salad made with finely cut onions, carrots, and coriander leaves mixed into rich, creamy yogurt. Altogether you get a full meal that will wake up taste buds you never thought you had!

The difference between Thalassery biryani and others is that it uses kaima/jeerakasala rice, which is a thin short-grain rice and is also called biryani rice in Kerala. The dish does not use basmati rice. Thalassery biryani uses a unique, aromatic, small-grain, thin rice variety named kaima, jeerakasala, or *jeeraka chamba* rice. This rice does not require presoaking, and water is only used to clean the rice. So after sufficient boiling, there will not be any water remaining in the cooking pot as it would have evaporated automatically.

Thalassery *falooda* is a regional variant of the Persian dessert. It has its origins from Parsis, who are half Persian and half Indian. This is a concoction of rose syrup, milk, and vanilla ice cream, laced with *cus cus* seeds and grass jelly. It is delicious on a hot day and can be a meal by itself if you are watching your waistline.

Malayalis Eating on Banana Leaves

Malayalis traditionally eat on banana leaves. The meals consist of white rice and other spicy accompaniments to add taste to the white rice, which on its own is bland. Rice is served on a banana leaf with a variety of vegetables, pickles, *papadum* (Indian crackers), and other regional condiments (usually sour, salty, or spicy). The banana leaf acts as a disposable plate and is not eaten.

Banana leaves contain nutrients such as a plant-based substance known as polyphenols or ECGG. This is also found in green tea. Polyphenols are natural antioxidants that fight free radicals and combat diseases.

It is believed that food placed on banana leaves will soak up nutrients such as polyphenols, enhancing the nutritional value of the meal. Typically, there will be two servings of rice. The first is served with gravy, side dishes, and other spicy accompaniments, while the second serving will be just rice with plain yoghurt as a cleanser for the palate.

In North Malabar, one special dish to begin an Onam sadhya is *papadam pasham*, which is squashed banana sprinkled with papadam crumbs (or Indian crackers) then tossed with cane sugar and a spoonful of ghee or clarified butter. This is how a traditional Onam meal begins, followed by the savouries of curries and rice.

Meals on banana leaves meals must be eaten with the right hand, and after a meal, the guest must fold the banana leaf inwards. This is supposed to be a sign of gratitude to the host, even if the host is a restaurateur.

When Kishen Left India

Kishen was just sixteen years old when he left the shores of Kerala, India, heading first to Myanmar (then Burma), where he worked as an assistant in a doctor's clinic before going to Singapore as a pioneer immigrant.

He arrived filled with dreams and was determined to make it all become a reality. He was brave and adventurous in wanting to build a good life for himself and to build a family and provide well to the best of his ability. He had an indomitable spirit to succeed and harness the best of his life. He came to Singapore in search of greener pastures and was optimistic, cheerful, and full of energy and high aspirations.

Kishen is a simple man but one with a sharp business acumen. He did not have a formal education but is a self-made man who mastered Hindi and obtained the equivalent of a degree in it. What he did go through was the education of life, and he put the lessons he learnt to good and wise use.

His earnings were modest in the beginning, but with wise and prudent investments, he planted seeds that saw him grow into a wealthy businessman. Slogging and toiling each day, he took a step forward every day of his life, and he soon used his savings to invest in a banana-and-mango plantation near the naval base in what is today Sembawang in Singapore.

The harvests were rich, and the plantations flourished, bringing in a decent income. The plantations were sprawled in acres with lush green vegetation. As the sun's resplendent rays peeked in, you could see the rich golden fruit hanging on the trees, ripe and ready to be picked and eaten. The sweet bananas and succulent mangoes all brought in money. The Japanese were occupying Singapore at the time, and they came to buy Kishen's natural products, as they were nourishing, nutritious, and splendid to the taste.

Kishen, being an amiable man, formed a good relationship with the Japanese who enjoyed the fruits of his plantations. It became a lucrative trade between Kishen and the Japanese during those dark days in Singapore.

Singapore during the Japanese Occupation

After the fall of the British on 15 February 1942, Japanese military forces defeated and conquered the combined British, Indian, Australian, and Malayan garrison in the Battle of Singapore. The Japanese occupied Singapore from 1942 to 1945, and it was renamed to Syonan, meaning 'light of the south'. During this time, resources were scarce, and people were encouraged to cultivate their own crops so that there would be sufficient food to eat. Most people grew their own vegetables, like tapioca.

Kishen's Marriage to Nandini

Kishen's next venture was to open a grocery shop. By then, he was considered a man of means, and he decided that it was time to find a suitable girl to marry. He returned to his homeland to do just that.

Shreiyaa's mother, Nandini, was a well-educated teacher in St Agnes College in Mangalore. By Indian standards at the time, age was pushing on. She was twenty-eight years old and, without looking at the face of Shreiyaa's father, had to approve to her betrothal; that was the culture during those days of arranged marriages. A rich man had come her way, but she was in deep anguish, as she had no choice in the matter— anguish, as she had to leave the shores of India for a land far away with a stranger who was to be her husband and companion for life.

In an auspicious wedding ceremony, the two were wed and set out to Singapore on a ship. Nandini's anguish and feelings of trepidation turned out to be unnecessary. She had married well to a devoted husband who was a decent and honourable man. She came from a good background, but her marriage elevated and enhanced her station in life in Singapore.

Their Faith: Lord Krishna

Shreiyaa's mother is a Hindu devotee of Lord Krishna and her father steadfastly follows the principles of Shri Ananda Guru. Though they now lived in Singapore, they jealously guarded their Indian heritage, traditions, and culture and practised them in Singapore.

Nandini, Shreiyaa's mother, was a devout Lord Krishna devotee who clung to her faith no matter what came her way and through all the struggles and uncertainties that she faced. Her undaunted faith was a guiding light that influenced Kishen and kept their spirit up at all times. This light was the cornerstone of all their successes and all the hurdles they had to surmount, and in later years, it influenced their children as well. Today, at the ages of ninety-six and eighty-eight, they still keep a picture of Lord Krishna in their shrine at home and venerate him with all their hearts.

The Caste System in India

Most societies are stratified; however, the extent of stratification differs in different societies. In India's Hindu society, the caste system is a system of stratification based on ascription rather than achievement, as is the case in most other societies. The English word *caste* originates from the Portuguese word *casta*, which means 'race', 'breed', or 'kind'. In India, *caste* is known as *jati* (literally translated as 'type').

The caste system of India discriminates some strata of people for being of lower type, such as the untouchables. The untouchables are considered the lowest form in the hierarchy of the caste system and had been ostracized and treated unfairly. The Brahmins are supposed to be the highest in the caste system, being of a priestly class, and the Kshatriyas, also an upper class, are said to be the warrior class. This unequal stratification of the caste system lead to the upper castes enjoying more privileges and opportunities compared to the lower castes, which is wholly unfair and wrong in essence.

Today there is still some residue of the caste system for those still caught in old traditions, though one can say safely that most of it is now eradicated and people have more equality and opportunities are available to one and all. The caste system of India is archaic and mostly redundant in this day and age.

A. W. Green says, 'Caste is a system of stratification in which mobility, movement up and down in the status ladder, at least ideally, may not occur.'

The British Raj and the Caste System of India

The subcontinent of India, now a large country, was once a colony under the British Empire. Hinduism is the main religion. However, India was steeped in malpractices of the caste system, where people were treated unequally, being stratified under a higher and lower caste. The British Raj contributed positively to eroding this archaic caste system by intermarrying. Women and children were treated with respect by their English husbands in an otherwise patriarchal society. Today the remains of the caste system still exist in certain parts of India. But most of the malpractices have been diluted, and there is more equality in this society.

Shri Ananda Guruji and the Caste System

Kishen was a founding member of the Shri Ananda Guru Mission in Singapore. It also goes by Oasis of Hope. It began when he and some like-minded devotees began meetings of devotion to the guru in an attap hut with a shrine and a lamp.

Today Shri Ananda Guru Mission in Bukit Timah is a well-respected philanthropic society that houses many unwanted and destitute old people, giving them dignity, love, care, and concern. The principles enunciated by Shri Ananda Guru have been preserved and upheld by the organization, and great inroads have been made for a better quality of life for the underprivileged. It has the other name of Oasis of Hope because it is a home for old people of all races in Singapore and does not discriminate at all. It is not meant for Indians alone; it is for all cross sections of society. As the name goes, it is an oasis of hope for the destitute, the old, the infirm, and the despondent.

The people who run the centre are compassionate and do their utmost to bring joy and laughter to the unwanted destitute who are in the evening of their lives. The building that houses these old destitute people is on a large, sprawling land with lush greenery and undulating hills nearby. The property was bought in this setting for a reason. This is so that they can go out on wheelchairs and enjoy the breeze and the sunshine and kiss the fresh air. Most old people who don't get sunlight suffer from sundown illness, which causes them to be disorientated in the night. The organization has trained nurses to take the old folks out to feel the sun so that it is a natural healer to sundown illness.

Ananda Guru, also known as Shri Ananda Guru, was a social reformer in India. He was instrumental in diluting the negative effects of the caste system and, to some extent, in eradicating it. He led a movement to reject casteism, reform society, and promote new values of spiritual freedom and social equality. He tried to uplift the downtrodden and the outcasts and is today considered one of India's wisest sages.

He was born into a family of the lower caste known as *Jaguns* in a time when people from such communities faced injustice in a society plagued with the caste system and its social ills. Jaguns were considered a lower social caste. Traditionally, they were agricultural labourers, small cultivators, toddy tappers, and liquor businessmen. Some were also involved in weaving and Ayurveda, which is one the world's oldest holistic healing systems. It was developed more than three thousand years ago in India, based on the belief that health and wellness depend on a delicate balance between the mind, body, and spirit. In Kishen's family, there were many physicians who practised Ayurveda.

Kishen was so dynamic that he also got involved in Singapore politics. At that time, Singapore and other Commonwealth countries, such as India, were fighting for independence from the British colonials. Kishen made his contribution by getting involved with the Malaysian Indian National Congress. He mixed and mingled with foreign dignitaries, like Subhas Chandra Bose and Jawaharlal Nehru, the first Indian prime minister of India.

The Children Are Born

Kishen and Nandini brought a son, Hemanth Kumar, and a daughter, Kajal Shreiyaa, into the world in 1958 and 1961. They became first-generation Singaporeans.

The 1950s and 1960s were a momentous time for Singapore. From self-government in 1959 to the merger with Malaya in 1963 and to independence in 1965, it was a period when Singapore was beset with uncertainties and challenges as it sought to carve its own destiny and identity.

The post-war generation was also trying to find its footing while searching for its future. Despite the political turbulence and social unrest, children growing up in those times were able to enjoy happy childhood years. The children of Kishen and Nandini were from their youngest days inculcated with their parents' sound values. As both parents were working, the children were raised by the maids Papa Patty and Achi, who were elderly and of Indian Muslim origin. Achi was like a grandmother to the children, while and Papa Patty was notorious for carrying the children precariously with her two fingers on their upper palates, which was apparently to remove the extra wind in their stomachs, and yet the babies were safe!

Chapter 2

Early Childhood

Their beginnings were modest. Shreiyaa's father worked for the British when Singapore was a colony. He worked at the naval base, now Sembawang, and her mother was a secondary-school teacher in Marymount Convent School. With her degree in botany, she taught English and biology. They stayed in the naval base's quarters, a two-bedroom house spacious enough for a family. These were black-and-white terrace houses, much smaller than the sprawling bungalows which the British officers lived in.

Those were majestic buildings set in the midst of sprawling gardens. Even today, if you took a ride to the end of Sembawang, it is quite a breath-taking sight, and this is what the British bosses of the naval base enjoyed with their families. There is also a church and a small beach from where you can see Johor Bahru, Malaysia. The beach was nothing to write home about, but it was garnished with a man-made garden frequented by young lovers.

There was also a club where the British used to down their beers and enjoy live music, and they grew accustomed to hearing the music of that time by Simon & Garfunkel, the Carpenters, the Bee Gees, and the Beatles.

It was a place for rest and recreation, socializing, and fun. They never got to visit this place; it was too high-end for them, and you needed to be rich to gain entry into this club for *ang mos* (Singlish for *white man* or Caucasian). In those days, the white man was considered rich and of the upper strata of life. They inevitably looked up to the British; after all, they had brought civilisation to Singapore, which was once only a fishing village. The British were then part of Great Britain, so we naturally looked up to their greatness!

As the children of working parents, they were left in the hands of Papa Patty and Achi, who tended to them. They were taught to begin and end each day with a prayer of thanks to the Almighty.

They had many good neighbours who were close to them, but they were closest to the Khoo family, a Chinese Teochew family from mainland China who, like their parents, had come to make a home and a new life in Singapore. They were Auntie Geok, Uncle Ah Chow, Ah Cheng (the elder daughter), Ah Sing (the younger daughter), and two sons whose Chinese names she cannot recall. They called them Padica Anan and Singapore Anan. They coined the name Padica Anan, which means 'the brother who is learned and reads a lot', because he was always reading a book and Singapore Anan because he always used to go into town, like Orchard Road, and in their little minds that meant he was going out into far Singapore! Anan means 'brother' in Tamil. This is what you call living the mix of a multicultural society in Singapore!

Every morning was a nightmare for her mother. Shreiyaa used to tug at her sari and weep endlessly before Nandini boarded her taxi to school to teach. Shreiyaa missed her mother and did not want her to leave her alone. It was a big melodrama, and she would have to be held back and cajoled. Their neighbour Auntie Geok would hear the wild screams of a wailing, anguished child and come out to calm the situation. Sometime after her mother had gone, Shreiyaa would brush her teeth (with help) and, still dressed in her pyjamas, go to see Auntie Geok to eat her toast and half-boiled egg for breakfast. There was a reason why she used to go over. As Indians, they did not have light *soy sauce*, which their neighbours had. Auntie Geok would put some on Shreiyaa's half-boiled egg, and it was delicious. Shreiyaa used to relish the same breakfast every morning with the love of Auntie Geok, who was always so inviting and kind to her. There were other neighbours, kids of their age, with whom they spent endless evenings playing, like Carol, Jane, Robert, and Danny Boy.

Shreiyaa's brother, Hemanth, was now in a prestigious kindergarten, Marymount Kindergarten, where he would go with their mother in the mornings, dressed in his navy-blue chequered shirt and blue shorts.

Time went on in the naval base quarters, and every Chinese New Year, they would enjoy the traditional reunion dinner with the Khoos, tucking into sumptuous authentic Chinese food. They ate happily as a family with no colour or race barrier.

The Chinese New Year reunion dinner is typically held on the even of the Lunar New Year. It is a time when family members reunite to celebrate this auspicious occasion as a family and enjoy a very large meal together.

The dishes that make up the meal each has a special significance: longevity noodles; *fatt choy* (black algae), which is believed to represent prosperity; a fish dish which should not be finished so that leftovers can be stored, symbolizing abundance for the year ahead; and so on.

Four chefs in Singapore were responsible for the contemporary dish that is known originally as *qicai yusheng* (seven-coloured raw-fish salad). In 1964, while trying to create a new signature dish to attract more customers to their restaurant, four chefs—Lao Yuke Pui, Than Mui Kai Yu, Hooi Kok Wai, and Sin Leung (known affectionately as the Four Heavenly Kings)—reinvented the dish and served it at their newly opened Lai Wah restaurant. Their aim was to improve the fragrance, colour, and flavour of yusheng while also giving it texture and depth through the addition of peanuts and crisps.

There is also the exchange of ang pows, which are red packets of money. This is supposed to represent good fortune coming in for the year and the promise of abundance for the family members. Children love these ang pows, and it is at this time that they get lots of money. It is traditional for unmarried members of the family to receive the ang pows rather than the married ones, but these days, to make it a merry occasion, almost everyone receives an ang pow!

On Onam, the Khoos would come over to eat their authentic Malayalam cuisine or sadhya, and it was such a joyous occasion. Even though Auntie Geok and Uncle Ah Chow have passed on, they still keep the tradition of exchanging their cultural heritage with these neighbours, and they still eat dinner with them for Chinese New Year and Onam. They have a great lifelong friendship of half a century and enjoy the memories of yesteryears and reminisce at their dinners with laughter in their hearts.

Onam is a traditional harvest festival celebrated in the state of Kerala, India, and anywhere that Malayalam communities have settled. It falls in the Malayalam calendar month of Chingam, which in the Gregorian calendar is sometime between August and September. It is typically a vegetarian spread of more than twenty dishes with accompanying pickles and other accompaniments prepared as labours of love by the women in the family.

At a sadhya, people eat seated on the floor and cross-legged in what Indians would call a lotus position practised in yoga. It is cardinal that you only eat with your hands and that, too, only with the right hand. No cutlery is used except for serving the food. The rice and dishes are spread on banana leaves, which serve as plates. With your right hand, you mix the dishes into the rice, make a small mound of food, and bend forward to take it into your mouth. Your hand acts as a spoon.

In their family, they broke the rule and served non-vegetarian food to accommodate the Khoos. In the early years, these occasions were celebrated in their respective homes, but as both families prospered, they now have the Chinese New Year reunion dinner at the Shangri-La in Singapore and the Onam meal either at the Rang Mahal at the Pan Pacific Hotel or at the Tandoor at the Holiday Inn. Chinese reunion dinners now always start with the Singaporean tradition of *lo hei* (or yusheng) to bring in all the blessings for good fortune for the new year.

Auntie Geok's Foochow Fish Balls

Whenever Auntie Geok made them, they knew it because they could smell the aroma from their home. Hemanth and Shreiyaa would cuddle up together and pray, 'Please, God, make Auntie Geok give us some!' And lo and behold, they would get a whole bowl by evening!

Fish balls are a common Chinese food made from minced fish paste. In Fuzhou, China, they include a minced-pork filling.

How to Make Foochow Fish Balls

Scrape the fish fillet until you get a paste. Marinate the minced pork with soy sauce and coriander leaves. Form into small balls. Take a portion of fish paste, and press it around each ball of mince pork to form a larger ball. Drop the finished **fish ball** into lightly salted water. Repeat until all **fish** paste and filling are used up. Bring some water to the boil, drop the fish balls into it, and cook for eight to ten minutes. They are best served in a light broth with plenty of green leafy vegetables. One bite and you will experience a burst of juiciness and sweetness of the ground-meat filling within.

Making these fish balls is no easy feat. These days, few people make them at home, preferring the convenience of ready-made offerings from the supermarket. But if you've ever had them home-made with loving hands, as Hemanth and Shreiyaa did as children, you would never choose to settle for the machine-made, mass-produced alternative.

Another dish that Hemanth and Shreiyaa, in their innocence, would pray for was the awesome dumplings and *bak chang* that Auntie Geok would make. She would make them with arduous preparation of wrapping the glutinous rice in lotus leaves and steaming them in a large cauldron over an open charcoal stove.

Once again, their prayers would be answered. They would get their share by evening, and they would ecstatically tuck it into them.

Now fifty-six years later, the second generation of Khoos still gives them bak chang. This is on the festive occasions of the Bak Chang Festival though.

Bak chang is a traditional Chinese food made of glutinous rice stuffed with different fillings and wrapped in bamboo, reed, or other large flat leaves. They are cooked by steaming or boiling. In the Western world, they are also known as **rice dumplings** or **sticky-rice dumplings.**

Bak chang (sticky-rice dumplings) are traditionally eaten during the Duanwu Festival (Dragon Boat Festival), which falls on the fifth day of the fifth month of the lunar calendar (approximately late May to mid June). Let me tell you a bit about the Bak Chang Festival, or Dragon Boat Festival.

Dragon Boat Festival

The Dragon Boat Festival (Duan Wu Jie) is also known as Duan Yang, which means 'Upright Sun' or 'Double Fifth'. Falling on the fifth day of the fifth lunar month around the summer solstice, the festival is also commonly referred to as the Fifth Month Festival amongst the Chinese. Its origins can be traced to southern China, and festivities include boat races and eating rice dumplings. The festival had evolved from the practice of revering the river dragon, to the commemoration of Qu Yuan, a third-century poet and political figure of the state of Chu in ancient China.

Legends and myths
River dragon

The dragon was initially viewed as the benevolent spirit of the waters. It exemplified the masculine principle or *yang* in the Chinese ideology of harmony. Among common folk, it was believed that the river dragon controlled the rain and was thus worshipped during the summer solstice. Requests would be made for a balanced rainfall—sufficient to ensure a good harvest, without over-abundance that would cause destructive flooding.

The early Chinese dragon had the head of a horse, the body of a snake, wings of a bird, and four or five legs. There would be five claws on each foot if it were an imperial dragon; otherwise there would only be four claws. Chinese mythology counts at least five sea-dragon kings as part of the Chinese pantheon. These divine immortals were later adopted by Chinese emperors as the imperial emblem, and thus the dragon became a symbol of power, wealth and prosperity.

Qu Yuan

Primitive worship of the river dragon was often practiced during the summer solstice. The Dragon Boat Festival was associated with Qu Yuan's story only in the second century. Qu Yuan was a councillor and patriotic minister who lived in the third century BCE in the state of Chu. In the midst of turmoil during this period of the Warring States, Qu Yuan had warned his king, Lord Huai, of the threat that the northern state of Qin posed to the southern Chu. However, political intrigue led Lord Huai to banish Qu Yuan instead. The ministry was left in the hands of corrupt statesmen and Qu Yuan helplessly watched his motherland decline. Depressed, he penned beautiful, patriotic poetry such as 'Li Sao' (an allegorical poem stating his political aspirations) and 'Jiu Ge' (or 'Nine Songs', adapted from the folksong style), which gained Qu Yuan great renown.

In 278 BCE, General Bai Qi led the Qin armies to occupy Ying (the capital of Chu), and destroyed the imperial palace. Several months later, on the fifth day of the fifth moon in 279 BCE, Qu Yuan, driven to despair, threw himself into the Mi Luo River.

Hereupon the legend varies. Some suggest that fishermen at the scene attempted to save their minister. Having failed, they sought to appease his spirit by throwing rice stuffed in bamboo stems into the river to prevent the fish from eating Qu Yuan's body. Others say that the rice offerings were snatched by a river dragon and the rice had to be bundled in chinaberry leaves instead and tied with five different coloured silk threads in order to be effective. The triangular rice dumplings, or *zong zi,* thus became entwined with the festivities. Another version tells of farmers rowing out in dragon boats in their attempt to save Qu Yuan. Hence, dragon boat racing[10] has been held annually on the fifth day of the fifth lunar month, in honor of the memory of Qu Yuan.

Dragon boat races

During the spring and autumn seasons, the fishermen of Wu (Jiangsu Province) and Yue (Zhejiang Province) used dragon-shaped boats to appease the river dragons. Dragon boat races are believed to have started between 770 and 476 BCE. In the state of Yue, King Gou Jian regularly trained his navy using boat races. It was during the Han Dynasty that dragon boat racing became a sport. The boats were long and narrow, with prows painted like a dragon's head. Noisy gongs and drums set the pace for the rowers. Flags would flap in the air while spectators cheered boats, gaily decked in lanterns, towards the finishing line.

The Khoos were the best takeaway gift of their stay in the naval base, as they are still friends today, more than fifty years later.

Gila Patty

The children used to play around the block, but there was this lady who had a mental illness. They called her Gila Patty, which means 'mad auntie' in a mixture of Malay and Tamil. She used to humour them as they made fun of her; she sang and danced, letting her long flowing hair down and screaming in a high-pitched voice. She was altogether harmless, but to them, she was the highlight of their day as she was abnormal and entertaining. Every evening, the children would wait for her and scream 'Gila Patty is here!' and roll into roaring gales of laughter. It all seemed very funny to them. The poor woman was oblivious to their opinion of her, but she joined in the fun in her abnormality and perhaps entertained herself too as she was an outcast to everyone else.

Uncle Roti

Another highlight of their day was Uncle Roti coming on his bicycle with the back laden with goodies. He sold freshly baked white bread with a lavish spread of divine *kaya* (coconut jam) and scrumptious ivory-coloured *sugi* cookies for just 5¢ each. They would wait for 5 p.m., when he arrived, and all of them would crowd around him and buy their delicious evening tea bites. The sugi cookies were so good that one day when Shreiyaa saw 50¢ on the Khoos' sewing machine, she took it in all innocence, thinking, *I am rich, and I can buy lots of sugi cookies when Uncle Roti comes at 5 p.m.* Unfortunately for her, her brother, Hemanth, found out and told her mother; fortunately for her, she learnt her first lesson on morality and ethics. She was made to give it back to Auntie Ah Geok and apologize. It was then that she realized that you can't steal to be rich. It was impressed on her that it was wrong and she had to be satisfied with just one sugi cookie. She was deeply saddened, but her mother had to discipline her. Her brother, Hemanth, just three years older than her, had an inherent sense of right and wrong from a young age, so he paved the way for early lessons of upright living for her.

Six Years Later

Many things happened. They moved out of the naval base, as their parents had prospered considerably. Shreiyaa started school at Marymount Convent, and they went as a family to Kerala, India, to their ancestral homes—Cherumana Nivas on her mother's side and Shantha Nivas on her father's side.

Their New Home, Their New Life

Her father now had a lucrative business of his own in the property market, and he shrewdly invested in some properties of high value in a prime location. He made some handsome profits during the property boom in Singapore. By now Shreiyaa and her brother had their own rooms, and they had three maids, a gardener, a driver, and two cars. One maid looked after her brother and her, the other was the cook, and the third was what was called the washerwoman, as in those days there were no washing machines. She washed clothes under a running tap and ironed them when they were sun-dried on a bamboo pole in the backyard of their home. They also had three dogs—Bobby, Julie, and Lassie. Their home was a large semi-detached house in the Thomson area. It was spacious, and life took a new turn as they prospered tremendously and enjoyed lots of luxuries.

Trip to Kerala

This was an exciting moment—their first trip to Kerala. When they landed in Madras (present-day Chennai), she was aware that the air they breathed was not so clean and the roads were crowded and dirty with cow dung. There were beggars everywhere, but this change of scene was an adventure despite the heat and dust. If you are of Indian origin, you can weather the storm because as the saying goes, 'You can take an Indian out of India, but you can't take India out of an Indian.' They went on a train to Thalassery and arrived in her mother's ancestral home. This huge palatial building was made of brick and dark-brown mahogany wood. At the front of the house, there was a sizeable brass container of water, which you were supposed to use to wash your feet before entering barefoot.

It had a large garden blessed with coconut trees that swayed languidly from side to side in the light breeze, lovely mango trees, and a vine of large passion fruits, the largest Shreiyaa had ever seen. Shreiyaa's grandmother, who was beautiful and fair as snow, made them cups of refreshing passion fruit juice to cool them down from the hot, humid weather, and this was indeed so welcoming. They met their grand-aunties, for whom they had brought a cartload of gifts of towels, perfumes, and soaps. For in those days, they could not get these things in India, or if they could, it was too costly from the man on the street, especially the brands they brought from Singapore. They had delicious roasted cashew nuts to munch, and they basked in the love of their paternal and maternal grandparents, who were so happy to see the children of Kishen and Nandini Venugopal for the first time.

They met so many relatives who kept feeding them non-stop. Shreiyaa remembers that all their grand-aunts were always dressed in pristine-white saris, as they had all been widowed by this time. For Indians, once you are widowed, you should only wear white as a mark of respect to your deceased husband.

Shreiyaa's earliest recollection is of her grand-auntie Mythili, who was disabled and sat in a wheelchair. She had been, in the earlier days, the principal of St Agnes College Mangalore. Immediately after she met her, she felt a divine connection with her, and she used to run up to her and kiss her all the time. Her grand-aunt loved her. One day when Shreiyaa was playing, she fell down and bruised her knee. It was nothing serious, but her grand-aunt waved her hand and called Shreiyaa over. Shreiyaa ran to her, and her grand-aunt put her hand on Shreiyaa's knee and wept to express her anguish because she had hurt herself. Shreiyaa used to pick bright-red hibiscus and yellow roses from the garden in front of the house and give it to her grand-aunt to express her love, and her grand-aunt appreciated it very much.

Homestyle Food

In Kerala, certain dishes are a given, and they are delicious.

Appam is a pancake made with a batter of fermented rice flour and coconut milk. In Kerala, you get authentic appam, which is infused with a hint of toddy (coconut liqueur). It is made in a special pan called an *appachatti*, which has a deep mould, so the appam comes out shaped like a little bowl. Crispy on the edges and fluffy in the centre, it is mostly eaten for breakfast in Tamil Nadu and Sri Lanka; it is eaten for dinner too.

Ishtu (Kerala stew) is what they ate with the appams. Vegetable ishtu or mutton ishtu is a classic side dish served in Kerala. This particular dish is a mix of vegetables cooked in coconut milk and spiced up with hot black peppercorns and is extremely good in taste. It requires potato as the main ingredient and is very simple to cook.

Thosai, or *ghee roast*, which is also a pancake, is sometimes filled with potatoes and mixed vegetables. This is eaten with white- or red-coconut chutney (the redness comes from chili powder and tomato puree). The stuffed thosais are known as masala thosai, and if you eat this for breakfast, you will not be hungry till at least 3 p.m.

Puris (also spelled *poori*) with her grandmother's fish curry—the taste of the fish curry is still etched in her mind. Puri is an unleavened deep-fried Indian bread, eaten for breakfast or as a snack or light meal. It is usually served with curry.

Kallamakkai (or mussels) are freshly picked from the rivers and made into a hot, spicy pickle. This is a delicacy of Thalassery and is considered the caviar of North Malabar. It is also pan-fried or prepared with rice balls. There is a an old wives' tale that you can only eat mussels in the months that have an *r* in them; otherwise they are poisonous.

Well Water Baths

One often-underappreciated health perk of rural living is unlimited access to a cleaner, more natural source of water: **well water.** The well was just outside the bathroom, which had a window with a rope on a pulley, with which they drew the water on a pail for bathing. The water was refreshingly cool, and it appeared to keep your whole body moist after the bath. If they looked into the well, it was deep, and they could see some fish swimming in it. What actually purified the water was the fish eating the algae and other toxic matter. It was a lovely experience, coming from Singapore and experiencing this rural lifestyle. It was magical to feel the fresh well water on their skin.

Bullock and Horse Cart Travel

They travelled by bull and horse cart in Thalassery, and all around were cows and goats roaming around. The roads were cut through mud paths. Most of the women were dressed in artistically designed saris of a multitude of colours, and the men wore kurtas (long shirts) and lungis (equivalent to a sarong), a floor-length linen cloth draped around the waist. Women sometimes wore pristine sweet-smelling jasmine flowers in their hair. They had a red dot between their eyebrows if they were married or a black dot if they were unmarried. *Bindi* is a Sanskrit word meaning 'point' or 'dot'. A bindi is a small ornamental, devotional dot applied to the forehead in Hinduism. In addition to the **bindi**, in **India**, a vermilion mark in the parting of the hair just above the **forehead** is worn by married women as commitment to the long life and well-being of their husbands.

They had a great time in India going back to their roots, and they returned to their homeland, Singapore, soaked in all their cultural and traditional heritage.

Chapter 3

Teenage Years

Their teenage years were glorious years of carefree living, travel adventures, and excitement. They discovered new dishes of the multicultural society in Singapore every weekend when their parents took them out for dinner. They ate Chinese, Indian, Malay, Eurasian, and English food at different restaurants but never drank alcohol, as it was banned in their home. They went to school—Shreiyaa at a renowned convent, the Marymount Convent School, and her brother to a Catholic boys' school, St Joseph's Institution. There was abundance in the home, as Kishen and Nandini provided well. Kishen and Nandini were devoted to giving their children the very best life.

Shreiyaa and Hemanth had lots of friends, and every year, their birthday parties were spectacular events. They were blessed with a holiday every year to many interesting places around the world. They went to many parts of India besides Kerala; Calcutta, Bombay, Goa, Cochin, Kashmir, Delhi, Benares, Khajuraho, Haridwar, and Rishikesh were some of the exciting destinations they travelled to as a family. They also travelled round Europe, England, Scotland, France, Germany, Switzerland, Holland, Austria, and Italy and also to Indonesia and Malaysia.

The world is a book, and those who do not travel read only a page. (Saint Augustine)

The family reads many pages of this 'book' and 'read' many lifestyles all over the world.

The Earth is filled with infinite experiences, wonders and once-in-a-lifetime opportunities. Imagine hiking through the verdant, kaleidoscopic Amazon rainforest, camping out underneath the aurora borealis in the Canadian tundra or meandering through an enchanting Kenyan village. Much education is experienced in a classroom or through a textbook; those avenues do get the job done, but they aren't nearly as fulfilling or effective as traveling the world is.

See the world, and broaden your cultural, intellectual, and spiritual education like you could never have imagined. (Leon Logothetis)

There are places in India that fascinated Shreiyaa during her teenage years.

Goa

The beaches of Goa are breathtaking, and you can feel the rays of the sun when you sit on the beaches. Shreiyaa remembers thinking eventually she would want to buy a house by the beach in Goa and be a beach bum, but it still hasn't happened!

Goa is blessed with scenic beauty of great magnificence, and the architecture of its temples churches and houses puts Goa in a central focus as a favourite place to holiday for travellers around the globe. It is known as the Pearl of the Orient.

Goa is more than beaches and bright sunshine; it has a soul which permeates its history and culture and some of the most natural scenery of India. People are also laid-back and happy-go-lucky. The place is full of Caucasian tourists finding some light in their lives, and amidst all this, you will find gypsies in their entire regalia or rich-coloured apparel and headdresses in every nook and corner. It is a place to relaxation from the taxing rat race of the world. It is a place to unwind and people to watch too, as everyone is in for fun and laughter. You will find musicians strumming away happily on their guitars. Streets are lined with shops selling ornate silver jewellery with precious gems along with T-shirts and kurtas of the sixties hippy culture. It is a place for lots of booze and even marijuana (though Shreiyaa never tried any of this). It is a place to escape from the harsh realities of life.

Real estate is of a high standard, and lovely condominiums in Condolim have inviting swimming pools. There is also the renowned Church of Saint Francis of Assisi with the tomb of St Francis Assisi, whose body has still not decomposed, a miracle of life indeed. It is a meeting point for the East and the West. And the Goans are very warm and friendly people.

They stayed at the Leela Palace, which was the most majestic, fabulous piece of architecture Shreiyaa had ever seen in all her life. The architecture is of Vijayanagar style, rich and opulent. The Leela Palace Goa is an award-winning luxury beach-and-riverside resort in South Goa. It is spread across seventy-five acres of lush lawns and features luxurious rooms and superb golf courses. The beach is within walking distance. You experience paradise on earth staying here. They had their fill of *bebinka*, a typical Portuguese dessert of lovely layered crepes richly laden with creamy coconut milk. They also had lots of seafood, which is a staple in Goa. The hot fish curry, the *rava* prawns, and rava red snappers were just delicious. These are large prawns and fish deep-fried in semolina batter, which is crispy on the outside and moist inside. It's so delicious the taste will forever be etched in your mind. Also, the fish and chips in Goa is better than what you find in London or Scotland.

Cochi

Cochin/Kochi is a modern city where shopping markets, cinema complexes, industrial buildings, amusement parks, marine drive, etc. are located. It is also the commercial and IT hub of Kerala. From time immemorial, Arabs, Chinese, Dutch, British, and Portuguese seafarers followed the sea route to Kochi and left their impressions on the town. The Chinese fishing nets swaying in the breeze over the backwaters, the Jewish Synagogue, the Dutch Palace, the Bolgatty Palace, and Portuguese architecture in Kochi enrich the heritage of Kerala.

The weather is tropical in Fort Kochi. It is hot and humid in the summer from March to June with the scorching sun's rays sitting on your skin and cold and wet when there are torrential rains between June to September. An ideal time to visit this place is between October and February. There is a ten-day carnival in December, and there is all that merrymaking and much to enjoy.

To get you around, you should ride the autorickshaws (or tuk-tuk). It can be bumpy if the roads are uneven, which can be quite thrilling, but on the overall, it's a lovely ride because you can look out and see shops and the architecture of churches and mosques in all their splendour.

The auto rides are fun and cheap, with the autorickshaw *walas* being most amiable and charming. They love tourists and will pander to you with such a friendly demeanour, because not only are they proud of their city but they also want to hear a word or two about where you come from. They all seem to be merrymakers who love their job of ferrying tourists to places of interest in Fort Cochin.

Shoppers' Paradise

A very rich history lies in the pretty, sensational streets of Fort Kochi. *Pretty* is an understatement to describe this peaceful, vibrant city in Cochin, Kerala, India. This scenic city is pulsating with vigour and gusto. The heartbeat of Fort Cochin is lined with a treasure trove of shops with the most exquisite and exotic brass and silver artefacts;

an array of beautiful and delicate colourful handwoven silk scarves; Kashmiri shawls; rich wall hangers studded with semi-precious gems; carpets; tapestry; and ornate jewellery. For the devout and ardent shopper, you will find a fairyland of gifts you can take back for your friends and relatives at very affordable prices. You can be sure you will not find them anywhere else in the world, as each piece of exquisite item is uniquely made with handwoven embroidery on tapestries, carpets, shawls, and scarves. The jewellery is opulent and tastefully designed and goes back generations to the times of the Mogul period in India.

For that, incredible India definitely earns top marks for its rich art and culture. You will find the zenith of unique designs in the streets of Fort Cochin; the shopkeepers don't annoy you because they are so sure of the perfection in their display of exotic Indian mementos, so bargaining is at a minimum. In many shops, prices are all regulated by the government of India to cater to the tourists. What you get, whatever it may be, is a perfect piece. Therefore, you can be sure of the highest integrity for the price you pay for the very best. However, there are shops where you can bargain and bring down the price too; it adds to the fun and joy in shopping, which is different from being in a stereotype modern shopping mall.

One of the main tourist attractions in Fort Kochi is the Chinese fishing nets. It is believed to have been originally installed by the Chinese from Macau in the fourteenth century. As you walk on the blissful beaches of Fort Kochi, you'll see friendly fisherman sitting along with wooden poles, making their catch for the day. They would wave out to you as you walk along the beach. It is best to go early at dawn or at dusk to catch the beauty of this scene, which makes a lasting impression on your mind.

They stayed at Koder House in Fort Kochi. Opposite the breathtakingly beautiful beach at Fort Kochi, Kerala, India stands a magnificent, rich, majestic wine-coloured three-storey heritage boutique hotel called the Koder House. You cannot miss it because the building makes a statement on the streets of Fort Kochi. Koder House is more than a heritage sight; it is an experience of a journey into the rich history of the Malabaris and the Jews of Kerala, which you must not miss if you come to Fort Kochi. Until recently, it belonged to the most illustrious Jewish family in Cochin, the Koders. This house had been a host to presidents, prime ministers, viceroys, ambassadors, Nobel laureates, Hollywood directors, and prominent dignitaries. This dwelling also finds a prominent place on INTACH's list of heritage sites, and a visit to Fort Kochi is considered to be incomplete without a visit to this historic site. Shreiyaa is proud to say that Koder House is owned by her cousin who has two other five-star hotels in Kochi.

Initially, Kochi was an obscure fishing village that later on became the first European township in India. The town was shaped by the Portuguese, the Dutch, and later the British. These cultural influences are seen in the many examples of Indo-European architecture that still exist here. Some of the well-known tourist attractions in Kochi are the Chinese fishing nets, Vasco House, Parade Ground, Cochin Club, Jew Town, Cherai Beach, etc.

Kashmir

Kashmir is the northernmost part of India. As you land from a plane, you can see the mountainous area, and the sight is far more scenic and prettier than the Swiss Alps. Emperor Jahangir was known to say that if there is paradise on earth, it is here in the Kashmir Valley. Women are so beautiful and fair-complexioned with naturally rosy cheeks. You will find wild daffodils and tulips growing here and fresh salmon in the lakes. It is believed that the maharajah passed an edict that foreigners were not allowed to buy land in Kashmir; that is why there is not much history of the British Raj in Kashmir. But in my view, if the British had their way, today Kashmir would not have been so trouble ridden and its beauty would still have been preserved instead of being war torn with the territorial conflict between India and Pakistan. The pollution caused by these conflicts have tarnished the natural beauty of Kashmir.

Dal Lake in Kashmir

Over fifteen kilometres around, Dal Lake is Srinagar's jewel, a vast sheet of water reflecting the carved wooden balconies of the houseboats and the misty peaks of the Pir Panjal mountains. Flotillas of gaily painted shikaras (gondola-like taxi boats) float around the lake, transporting goods to market, children to school, and travellers to delightful houseboats inspired by originals from the Raj era.

If you get up early, you can paddle out to see the floating flower and vegetable market: a colourful spectacle.

Houseboats on Dal Lake

Those houseboats are lovely by-products of a bit of legal artful dodgery. Under the terms of the nineteenth-century maharaja who had control of Kashmir, the British were not allowed to build houses on his territory. But boats were not houses, and lakes were not lands, so the officials of the Raj continued to spend summer at the temperate Kashmiri paradise, living there in waterborne mansions.

Shreiyaa's family stayed first at the Royal Houseboat. Outside, its eaves were trimmed with lacy fretwork. Inside, the walls were panelled with cedar, so the very air you breathed was aromatic. There were chandeliers everywhere. There were silk carpets. There was massive, intricately carved walnut furniture. There was a veranda with cushioned benches, ready for an afternoon snooze.

There was Hassan, the shikara boy, who would paddle you around the lake in a canopied boat painted with the colours of marigolds and delphiniums and pomegranate. And there was Mr Din, the boat captain, always spruced in his white jacket and crocheted skull cap; he will called them sir or madam and brought them a gilt-rimmed cup of tea flavoured with cardamom or served a feast of cinnamon-scented mutton and yogurt-dressed cauliflower on the flat roof overlooking the acres of lotus flowers, which were what you got here instead of a garden. They had stuffed dal parathas and other exotic curries of Kashmiri origin on the houseboat, and it warmed up their tummies in the cold winter at the Dal Lake.

A Marriage Proposal on Dal Lake

When they went to the houseboat on Dal Lake, the tour guide, Gulam, a Muslim Kashmiri, asked Shreiyaa to marry him. She was just fifteen, but the proposition was very attractive to her at that age. She would get four houseboats to her name. She would be his second wife, and he promised to give her Rs.10,000, which at that point in time seemed like a lot to her. Her mother was aghast when she told her! She told her not to talk to him, and she kept her eyes on Shreiyaa like a hawk throughout their stay. It was obvious destiny had other plans for Shreiyaa other than being the wife of a Kashmiri in Kashmir!

Apples of Kashmir

The apples of Kashmir are just simply awesome. You get them in extremely large sizes and small sizes, and they are juicy sweet like nectar and just lovely.

When they were in Kashmir, they ended up eating only apples for a meal at lunch and munching on walnuts. Kashmir is known as the fruit bowl of India with unique and crunchy apples which are indeed so delicious to taste. It is the prime source for apple production in India, and its apples are far superior to those from any other parts of the world. Its shape, taste, and quality and the varieties you get make it totally outstanding and better than those from anywhere else in the world. Its geographical setting and the weather are conducive to producing by far the best apples of the world.

Get Your Dirty Hands Off Me

In Gulmarg, Kashmir, Shreiyaa was so amazed by the beauty of this place. She jumped on a horse to gallop away. Her mother had to keep up and chase her. As her mother was clad in a sari, she had difficulty mounting the horse, so the Muslim Kashmiri guide tried to give her support by pushing her on to the horse with his hands on her buttocks. She yelled, 'Get your dirty hands off me!' Both the guide and Shreiyaa chuckled at the funniness of it.

Gulmarg's legendary beauty makes an indelible impression on you.

It was originally called Gaurimarg by shepherds, and its present name was given in the sixteenth century by Sultan Yusuf Shah. The sultan was inspired by the sight of its grassy slopes and fields of fragrant wild flowers. Emperor Jahangir once collected twenty-one different varieties of flowers from this place. Today, Gulmarg is not just a mountain resort of outstanding beauty, but it also boasts the highest golf course in the world, at an altitude of 2,650 metres. It is also the country's prime winter ski resort. You can feast your eyes on the marvellous mountainous area with snow-capped mountains against a horizon of lush greenery glazed on the blue mountains. The whole scenery is enchanting indeed, and the air is cool, fresh, and clean. It seems as if you could touch the clouds with your bare hands—simply breathtaking. This is one spot in the world that you can marvel at the works of Mother Nature and think, *What an amazingly artistic creator we have!* The natural beauty of this place is beyond all description indeed.

Another Marriage Proposal at Taj Mahal in Delhi

Even though of Indian origin, as a Singaporean, when Shreiyaa goes to India, she is not in any way Indian, so to speak. The Indians know she is a foreigner. At this abode of love, Shreiyaa had another marriage proposal from Amjad Ali, a passer-by from Pakistan visiting the Taj. When he came to talk to her, he left a note. Her mother had her antennae out, and she read the note, which said, 'I love you. Do you want to marry me?' From then on, her mother watched Shreiyaa's every step, and she could not even be lightly flirtatious with these foreigners. It was clean fun, and she just seemed to be the centre of attention, as she was dressed differently from the typical Indian girls.

> **Taj Mahal**. An immense mausoleum of white marble, built in Agra between 1631 and 1648 by order of the Mughal emperor Shah Jahan in memory of his favourite wife, the **Taj Mahal** is the jewel of Muslim art in India and one of the universally admired masterpieces of the world's heritage.

The travel she did as a teenager brings a treasure trove of happy and pleasant memories. All the lovely times she spent with her parents and her brother are indeed very close to her heart. The rich experience is always preserved within her in a very vivid way.

Soulful Lessons from Kishen and Nandini

Kishen and Nandini were down to earth in their upbringing of their children. Though they had a privileged background, they were always told to remember the poor, the sick, the dying, the downtrodden, and the underprivileged. On their trips to India, they also were exposed to poverty and squalor. Shreiyaa used to weep when she saw this scene, and her parents would readily give them money to give to the beggars on the street.

Though this came from their hearts, in India begging is a profession, and sometimes the beggars had bosses, who would take the money away from them. It was a cut-throat profession. The beggar to the Indian citizen was different for the tourists, who came with a loaded pocket. Indian citizens knew that these beggars were not as innocent as they appeared.

When they were at a Kali temple in Kolkata, their uncle from India, Uncle Ramshankar, warned them not to give any money to the beggars.

They did not heed his advice. Before long, the beggars crowded around their car, like bees to a hive, and would not let their car pass as they formed a line blocking the front and back of the car, screaming and wailing for money handouts. It was a nightmare for the family, and they had to sit still and not give anything until the crowd of beggars finally decided to leave, as they knew they were not getting anything more from them!

Other Lessons from Nandini

Nandini was a teacher, and she used to teach English.

Their lessons were different and unique. Every weekend, they had to go to the reservoir or the park to see the sunrise or sunset, the lush greenery, and the mirror reflection of them in the puddles of water on the reservoir. They had to do creative writing about what they saw and translate this into words in an essay to improve their English. They were also made to read encyclopaedias and magazines like *Tell Me Why*, jot down words that they did not understand, and look them up the dictionary. They had to have a vocabulary book of their own. This was how she polished up their use of the English language.

Supporting Mother Teresa in Kolkata

Their parents deeply admired Mother Teresa and her saintly pursuits. Every month, their parents diligently sent a humble contribution to her organization in Kolkata, and Nandini even attended Mother Teresa's funeral. It was from these acts of kindness that they learnt as children to be compassionate to the sufferings of others and to help those who needed a helping hand.

A Dod Dies in an Accident

One poignant scene that touched Shreiyaa's heart and is forever etched in her mind was when Roderick, their neighbour's dog, a huge Alsatian, died in a road accident. They heard a loud bang, and when they ran to the road, they saw Shreiyaa's brother, Hemanth, in his white school uniform, in a puddle of blood. They were naturally shocked and distraught. Roderick was bleeding profusely. When they asked her brother what he was doing, he replied, 'The dog is going to die. It is afraid, so I am holding its hand!'

Lord Krishna Statue Comes to Their Garden

Nandini had green fingers, and every plant she nurtured would spring into flowers, fragrant and beautiful. She had a dream of a great garden that she could landscape, and one of her dreams was to have a statute of Lord Krishna in it. Uncle Achen was Kishen's boss and a very rich man. He knew of Nandini's aspirations. Though he was a Catholic, in his home, he had a huge life-sized Lord Krishna statute because he had taken over the home from a Hindu owner. When he was moving house, he gifted the statute to Shreiyaa's parents, and this was indeed a momentous event in their lives.

The statute weighed three tons and was a magnificent work of art. At the time, they were part of a religious organization, the Temple of Fine Arts. All the members came over, dug a deep hole in front of the garden, and it was hoisted by a huge crane with much difficulty and put into the ground. It took a long time, and all sang praises to Lord Krishna in the form of bhajans (Hindu hymns), and the statute finally settled in very well. They celebrated with vegetarian lunch by a caterer for all who came to support them. They are still part of this religious group but are not very active. They still, however, keep in touch with the members.

Nandini who was a botanist. She landscaped the garden with pebbles and plants such as exotic *Vanda Miss Joachim* orchids, *cattleya* orchids, and *golden showers* on one side of the garden, and on the other side, she had a rose garden that seemed like one in England. *Mr Lincoln* was one of her mother's favourite rose plants that grew into a huge red rose flower, and they would make home-made perfume out of it. The plants were all in full blossom all the time. There was an arch with rich orange *Bohemia*s that grew into a thick herbaceous vine. They had *bougainvillea*s of different colours and fuchsia-pink *Japanese roses* creeping out of the rock garden's retaining wall. There was a pond of divine *lotus* floating with *water lilies* daintily dancing in the breeze.

In the pond were large goldfish swimming happily and small tortoise too. On the other side of the garden was a fountain with green foliage around it, and it was a spectacular sight indeed. In the backyard of their home, they had a coconut tree, a mango tree, and a banana tree, which yielded rich harvest of fruits during the season. And on the side of the garden, Nandini had a hand in growing vegetables and herbs, like ladies' finger, chillies, pumpkin, basil, and mint.

Nandini's dream had come true, and from then on, she pledged to be a full-fledged vegetarian as a symbol of compassion to animals and as a sacrifice towards prayers that her children would come up well in life. They were brought up going to prayer meetings called satsangs, where they sang bhajans and chanted gayatri mantra.

The meaning of the Gayatri mantra is as follows:

> We contemplate the glory of Light illuminating the three worlds: gross, subtle, and causal.
> I am that vivifying power, love, radiant illumination, and divine grace of universal intelligence.
> We pray for the divine light to illumine our minds.

Every Friday, Shreiyaa would wash the statute of Lord Krishna in the garden with a hose, pluck flowers from the garden, make a garland and put it on him, and pray to him to bless her with a good husband. There was a twist in her fate in this respect eventually that hurt her deeply.

Going Overboard with Kindness

There was this old lady bent double who used to come to the gate at their home and show them the vegetables she had to sell. They were all rotten and withered up. Someone told Shreiyaa that she was chased out by her daughter-in-law and she had no means to live. Shreiyaa decided since they were rich, she should help her. She took $50 from her father's wallet without him knowing and gave it to her in exchange for a red chilli with a worm in it. She got into lots of trouble with her father when he found out what she had done, and that was the end of that. However, the seed was in her to go out and help the poor from a young age till this day. Shreiyaa still does so, leaving very little for her own needs.

Their Dogs

Bobby had a face of a cow. She was beautiful and absolutely charming. Her mannerisms were so pleasant and appealing. One day she was limping and cowered into a corner, groaning in pain. She had had an accident and had broken her leg. Shreiyaa wept uncontrollably and called her father in the office, saying he had to come back and tend to the dog. He just told her to apply Tiger balm on the dog's leg. Later on, they took the dog to a veterinarian surgeon, who said she had to be put down. Shreiyaa kicked up a big fuss and cried so much that the vet decided to operate on her leg and put in a steel splint; she lived with them for another seventeen years. When she eventually died, she had a very blessed burial, with Shreiyaa's father praying for her soul and putting flowers on her grave.

Julie was a very intelligent mongrel. One day Nandini bought orchid plants and left them in the car that was parked outside the house for a long time. Julie faithfully stood by the plants, guarding them, until her mother realized the plants were outside the house.

Lassie was a lovely terrier who died eventually of cancer. She was very furry with a mixture of brown-and-ivory fur and was a quiet dog who sat prettily and did her own thing, like eating and guarding the house. She had a lovely temperament and gave no trouble to anyone right to the end.

Spotty was very beautiful to look at but had a very bad character. She was vicious and spoilt. She would sit on the sofa and watch television in the evenings, hugging the cushion. When they told her to go, she would bark and show her front canine teeth to them and threaten to bite them. She also had lots of boyfriends who would come to mate with her; when they did, they broke the orchid pots of Shreiyaa's mother. In the end, her mother decided to give her away, saying she was a cheap bitch! After all their dogs died, they did not have any more. Their mother did not like their fur on their furniture. Their mother gave an ultimatum to all of the dog lovers that they had to choose between having a dog or a mum, so in fact there was no choice at all.

Clean Fun with Friends: A Cobra Is Stretched

Hemanth and Shreiyaa had many neighbourhood friends. They were Denise, Mark Micheal, Angela, and Cheng San. At the back of Faber Gardens was a kampong, or village. This was before it developed into the condominiums that are there now. It was up on a hill, and so every weekend, they would get together and go 'mountain climbing'. There were wild sweet potatoes, tapioca, and sugar cane growing there. There were also jackfruit trees with an abundance of fruits. They would climb these trees and dig for tapioca and sweet potato and bring it to their tree house nearby, which they had built with planks and attap. In it, they would light a flame and toast the tapioca and sweet potato and just have good fun.

One day, Shreiyaa fell into a mud drain and could not get out. Her brother and friends had to dig her out of the mud drain, and she was covered with mud. They were so afraid of getting a beating for this that they asked all the neighbours to allow them to use their garden hose to wash away the mud so that their mother would not find out what they had gotten up to, but no one obliged. So they came home all muddied, and their mother told them to take a bath.

After the bath, they sheepishly asked their mother, 'When are you going to beat us for our wrong?'

She answered, 'Eat your lunch and get some strength first!'

It was her sense of humour because they did not get a beating in the end.

On another day, Denise and Mark found a huge ten-foot-long black python. Do you think they were scared? Shreiyaa was! Denise was very daring and held its head at one end, and Mark held its tail. They both pulled it and stretched it. My word, that was so brave, but in the end, they let the reptile go into the drain and no one knows what happened to it after that.

'Penchuri [Thief]! Catch her!'

This became the last time Shreiyaa ever decided to steal anything. At the back of Faber Garden near the kampong was a high retaining wall, and below was a succulent bunch of red-skinned bananas hanging from a tree. Her friends Beatrice and Andre let her down so badly. She went on a bicycle and told them she would pick the bananas and share it with them, and they agreed to this plot. Just as she took a stick to pick the bananas, they started shouting, '*Penchuri! Penchuri!* Catch her!' To her shock, an old man with a huge pole came running to hit her. In the heat of the moment, instead of quickly riding away on her bicycle, she threw the bicycle in one corner and ran for her life. She returned one hour later; the man was gone, and she took her bike back. Beatrice and Andrea had just wanted to have some fun at her expense, but they became her lifelong friends. Beatrice has moved on, but Shreiyaa treasures Andrea, as she is one of the greatest gifts of her life. Today, fifty years later, she is still her a friend, almost a sister, who has been with Shreiyaa through thick and thin, through the good or the ugly.

SUCHITTTHRA SHREIYAA LAKSHMI VASU

'One Ice Kachang, Five Spoons Please'

Ice *kachang* is something children in Singapore love, especially to cool off in the hot, humid weather of Singapore. It is made up of ice shavings; boiled, sweetened red beans; green jelly; and sweet syrup drips on the mountain of ice shavings. One day Andrea, Beatrice, and Shreiyaa went to the local market with their brothers, Hemanth, Bernard, and John. None of them had enough money to buy a bowl for themselves, so they asked 'One ice kachang, five spoons please!' so they could share. Mind you, ice kachang is very cheap, but all they could afford was one bowl with five spoons!

Fresh Orange Juice and the Gangster

On the same day, they also requested for freshly squeezed orange juice for all five of them. They legitimately paid the old lady serving them, but in her absent-mindedness, the old lady insisted they did not pay for it. An argument began, and they insisted that they had paid. Then all of a sudden, the old lady's son—a man of very large frame with tattoos all over his body—approached them. They could tell he was a gangster.

All of them got scared, as they were growing up at a time when secret—society gangsters were active. They decided not to argue as the problem could escalate, and in their fear, they laid all the money they had on the table and ran for their lives!

Secret societies in Singapore are generally Chinese in origin, and there is a historical reason for this. Owing to difficult and onerous conditions in South China, there was a large exodus of Chinese from Fukien and Kwantung provinces who migrated to South East Asia. All came to Singapore and brought with them their religions and customs, and many also brought their triad activities and traditions. Triad lodges were created so that migrants would have a place that felt like home. They had their own sense of integrity, and triad practices were maintained so that these secret societies grew and flourished.

The migrant population grew in leaps and bounds, and soon the triads began to set up protection rackets. Although the secret societies were linked and united by violence, extortion, and vices, they also played a part in building the social fabric of early Chinese migrants in Singapore. In present-day Singapore, secret-society activities have radically decreased.

Driving Mr Suaidi, Our Malay Tutor, Up the Wall

At school, they all had to study a second language, and it was compulsory to pass it for their PSLE (Primary Six Leaving Examination). They were studying Malay. They were all poor at the language, so Mother Kevin, a statuesque nun of Irish descent, who was their principal, decided to invest in giving them all extra Malay tuition. It was a gift, but they were plain horrible to Mr Suaidi. They would draw love signs, like a heart with an arrow, on his seat with chalk, so when he got up, that image in chalk would be imprinted on his backside. They would roar with laughter, and he would not know what was going on. They would put grass and salt into the petrol tank of his scooter so that his bike would stall. The poor man suffered under them convent girls, and then he complained. When Mother Kevin asked them who did it, all of them would all look sheepishly down as if they were innocent, and she just gave up on whom to punish, as she could not make out whom the culprits were. Finally, in tears, Mr Suaidi resigned! Their mission was accomplished—no more extra tuition in Malay!

Junior College Days

Shreiyaa went to St Andrew's Junior College, and it was here that she met some of her lifelong friends. After almost forty years, they still chat to each other on WhatsApp, sharing lots of laughter and wisdom as they go along. Their friendships are all platonic now—although all those years ago, on prom night, there were some secret love affairs and smooching in corners during the slow dancing. These are secrets best kept, as they have all moved on and some are happily married to other partners in life. Their identities need to be protected. Most of them are in very respectable jobs and are well placed in society.

One of the standing jokes they all always laugh about is when Andrea was in a mathematics class. Rajan was blocking her view of the blackboard, and Andrea asked him to move a bit so she could see better. He replied in Singlish, 'Why your mother born you so short!' That was so hilarious, and to this day, they laugh about it.

Another unfailingly hilarious moment was when Mr Keong, their history lecturer, was teaching. Every time he paused, the boys would play a musical-box tune. He would get confused and ask the students in the lecture hall if they could hear any music, and everyone would say no. In the end, he got distraught, thinking he was getting old, and he stopped the class, saying he was not feeling well! It was done in good fun; they were naughty, but not malicious!

Young Adulthood

Shreiyaa and her brother went to England for higher studies. He went to Manchester and she to London. She initially went to do journalism but moved on to read law, as she wanted something more challenging. Her brother read economics in Manchester.

Introduction of Spirits and Anglicisation

Do you remember that Shreiyaa said alcohol was absolutely banned in their home? Well, her brother, Hemanth, was in England a year before she went there for higher studies. Kishen and Nandini gave them a wonderful, happy holiday round Europe. They ate Western food, like a typical English breakfast with bacon and eggs and kippers, Italian pasta, Swiss fondue—the whole works. Hemanth told them, 'In Rome, do as the Romans do.' So they had exotic wine and expensive champagne, and they loved it. This began their anglicized lifestyle and the introduction of spirits into their diet. They drank champagne on the River Rhine in Germany, ate blini crepes with beluga caviar and sour cream in Paris, and had lots of Western cuisine. It was all so invigorating to their spirits to enjoy the Western exposure and culinary culture.

Chapter 4

The Love

The Venugopals had close family friends, also Malayali, from Singapore. Three of their six sons were sent to England for higher studies. The Chandrans came from a rich background. While in Singapore, Shreiyaa and Hemanth used to frequent the home of the Chandrans, who stayed in a big bungalow in Kheam Hock Road with a private swimming pool, a private squash court, and a full-fledged gym. It was a palatial home with seven bedrooms and five bathrooms and their taps in the bathrooms had gold-coloured rims. They also owned big cars, like Mercedes Benz, BMWs, and a Bentley. And they were well known for their mega wealth. Their family became well acquainted with the Chandrans and had what seemed a strong and lasting friendship.

Shreiyaa had her eye on the eldest son, Surendran. She admired him from afar, but in her heart, she wished he would love her and marry her eventually. As fate would have it, Surendran too was attracted to Shreiyaa but kept it to himself.

In London Shreiyaa embarked on journalism studies, while Surendran pursued law studies. He would always make sure Shreiyaa was safe, calling her by phone and asking if she needed anything and telling her she could depend and count on him if she ever felt lost. With his encouragement, she dropped out of journalism and pursued law studies too.

There was a mutual attraction in mind and spirit. Surendran was a man full of personality, was tall and handsome, and had a distinguished beard. From these casual telephone calls, soon love blossomed. Surendran started bringing beautiful red roses for Shreiyaa whenever they met, and soon he was taking her to see West End productions, like *Evita, Cats*, and *Jesus Christ Superstar*. There were the romantic dinners in high-end restaurants at Leicester Square in London and strolls around Trafalgar Square, Oxford Street, and Covent Garden. They started by holding hands and ended up falling deeply in love with each other. They became inseparable after some time of courtship. This was her first and only love, and she gave her all to Surendran, who looked after her as if she were a tender flower. He gave her joy and happiness, dispelling the loneliness of being in London and away from her parents for the first time in her life. He was enormously sensitive to her feelings and was extremely caring and devoted to all her needs, and she fully reciprocated. It was love—a sweet, innocent, and fresh young love to be cherished for a lifetime.

Surendran was the most loving and warm human being that she had ever met, and he lavished her with expensive gifts, like branded perfumes, ostentatious jewellery, beautiful flowers, and expensive dinner dates. He dated her in style and in the manner of a perfect and first-class gentleman.

She was sure in her heart and without a doubt that this was the man she wanted to be her husband. Surendran was also sure that Shreiyaa was his dream lady love. Their romance continued for a year. It was a fairy-tale romance—Surendran buying her handmade chocolates from Thorntons at Covent Garden, going to the cinemas, going on long walks, holding hands in the woods, and exploring parks and gardens.

Being so in love and away from the control and guidance of their parents, they adopted the Western way of life and moved into a rented apartment in Highgate, North London, which was unlike the Hindu principles they had both been brought up on. Initially, Shreiyaa had guardians looking after her in London, Professor and Mrs Jones, but on their encouragement, she plucked up the courage to move in with Surendran. In any case, here was her man, who was devoted to her and responsible in taking very good care of her. It was also an acceptable way of life in England and in the West.

Each of them dreamed of a life together and growing old together. She will always remember how one day when she was upset about something, Surendran took her to Hampstead Heath in the summer and the fields were covered with yellow daffodils fluttering gaily in the breeze. It was magically romantic to walk through the fields, with tulips and sweet peas filling the air with fresh summer fragrance. Dry leaves were dancing in the summer breeze before landing gently on the fresh green grass below. Walking through the natural beauty of Hampstead Heath was a blissful experience.

The house they rented was an old Victorian building converted into apartments along Archway Road. It was beautiful and large, carpeted in peacock blue, and had two open fireplaces. During the cold winter months of their one year of courtship, they used to sit by the fireplace, toast marshmallows and chestnuts, and nestle up to each other in a state of bliss. Archway Road had a Hindu temple on it, and they used to go there on Friday evenings to pray for blessings in their relationship. Shreiyaa was sure that the Lord Krishna statue in their garden had answered her prayers for a good husband.

For her twentieth birthday, Surendran surprised her with a birthday party with friends and a beautiful sapphire-and-diamond set of jewellery. Surendran loved her to the ends of the world and adored the ground she walked on so much that he would have spent his last dollar on her. On weekends and through different seasons, Surendran used to take her to the beautiful parks and gardens of London. He was good at photography, and he used to take pictures of Shreiyaa, develop them, and display them in a room he had dedicated to her image. For him, there was no woman more beautiful than she was, and she adored him and leaned on him for strength. He was a source of joy and comfort to her in every sense of the word, and she loved him with all her heart and with all of her.

In the winter of 1981, they went on a holiday to Cumberland Lodge, a gift and treat given to them by Professor and Mrs Jones. Lo and behold, their stay in Cumberland lodge was magical, as it was a white Christmas. The snow-covered fields were indeed a pleasant and spectacular sight and experience. They stayed indoors, sang Christmas carols by the open fireplace, and enjoyed an English feast of roast lamb, parboiled potatoes tossed in butter, Brussel sprouts, squash, toad in the hole, and sweetbread and butter pudding and cream for dessert. The meal ended with Irish coffee and an assortment of exotic cheeses with crackers.

Cumberland Lodge is a seventeenth-century Grade II listed country house in Windsor Great Park located three and a half miles south of Windsor Castle. It is located in a magnificent setting surrounded by natural chestnut trees and is now used by a charitable foundation which holds residential conferences, lectures, and discussions concerning the burning issues facing society. The primary beneficiaries are university students, 4,000 of whom visit the lodge each year. The Queen is its patron and has granted the foundation sole occupancy of the house.

Before they knew it, one year of fairy-tale courtship and idyllic romance passed. They had to go back for summer holidays to Singapore. They had decided to wed and had initially planned to do so in England and had even applied for a marriage license. But they decided to get the blessings of their parents, who were in Singapore. Shreiyaa remembers saying to Surendran, 'I am sure there will be no in-law problems, as our families are great friends.' But what was to come was completely the opposite of what they had anticipated.

Warning: Get your tissues out. You are entering painful chapters of Shreiyaa's life.

But all that happy life as a child and teenager turned to tragedy, pain, and anguish. A failed one true love broke her spirit and her mind.

Heavy and Severe Opposition to Marriage by Both Parents on Both Sides

Both families, when they heard about their love, were adamantly opposed to the marriage. There was a lot of fighting on both sides and no peace at all. Still they held on, insisting that they wanted to get married, as they were happily in love.

Surendran's mother was furious and rejected Shreiyaa, and Shreiyaa's parents retaliated and rejected Surendran. Mrs Chandran threatened to commit suicide if Surendran married Shreiyaa. She also made fun of her in a mean and nasty manner whenever they met. The couple were caught in the crossfire but put their foot down about getting married and did not budge from their plans to make a life together.

Shreiyaa could not believe anything that was happening. She had always gotten what she wanted in life, and this was perhaps the first challenge and episode of pain for her. Surendran kept promising her that all would be all right in time.

Their mothers went to see an astrologer, as it was normal for Hindus to consult an astrologer to see if there was a match and whether the marriage would work. To the shock of both mothers, the astrologer said that the marriage would not work out, as it was not a right match. Even then, Shreiyaa and Surendran decided not to believe the astrologer as the reality was, they were deeply in love.

Engagement

Finally, they got engaged, but the whole idea of marriage was without any good feeling or blessings from both sets of parents. Kishen and Nandini tried to protect her by asking her to back off, but her feelings were too intense to be reasoned with. Though she loved her parents, she could not back away from Surendran, as he was the love of her life. Mr and Mrs Chandran were wholly hostile to her and her parents and were very unwelcoming of and callous to their young love. They did not have a daughter of their own and had no understanding of a young girl's feelings and the sentiments of parents who doted on their daughter whom they brought up as a princess!

At a huge function with lots of important guests, they got engaged at the Shangri-La Hotel. It was in a garden setting with lovely music in the background, all paid for by Shreiyaa's parents, as this was the tradition in Indian families. None of the guests who arrived to rejoice in the union could have guessed at the nightmare behind the scenes. Everyone thought this was an ideal match, as the couple came from a high station in life; everything seemed right, and nothing appeared amiss.

Two Weeks Later

The marriage registration was to take place, and the two families were in a heated exchange of harsh words. On the day of the registration, both families were not speaking to each other. Only Mr and Mrs Chandran came, and they made the rest of their family boycott the registration ceremony. It was initially agreed to that lunch was to be celebrated at the Kashmiri Restaurant, but after the registration, Mr and Mrs Chandran whisked Surendran away from his new bride and refused to let him join the lunch celebrations. Surendran wept inconsolably, being helpless at this wreckage done to their love and dreams. Surendran was still financially dependent on his parents and was afraid to put his foot down and stick up for his bride. His friend Peter, who was there, cried too, saying to her, 'It was only my second marriage that worked out.' As his parents pulled him away from his young sobbing bride, Surendran said in between his sobs, 'At least we made it to get married. I will make it up to you in England.' This was such a bad omen on one's wedding day, and in her heart, she knew this would not work out eventually.

They were all horrified by this event. Kishen and Nandini did not know what to do, as they could not imagine that the Chandrans could be so downright cold, cruel, and brutal. Mr and Mrs Chandran were awfully rich. The extent of their wealth was beyond all imagination, and the children were easily bought over by their mother, who ran the household like a general in an army. She also had a weak, henpecked husband by her side. Money had gone to their heads, and they ruled in all matters no matter how callous. They had too much pride and not an iota of human compassion or kindness in them. They behaved like a mafia gunning down their victim mercilessly. They did this to a young girl who had not committed any crime except to have fallen in love with their eldest son. Hemanth and her eldest cousin, Rajan, held her hand throughout, telling her not to be afraid. Her dreams were shattered on her wedding day, her spirit was killed, and her heart raced. She and her family were distraught and in shock.

She did not see Surendran till 10.35 p.m. that night, when he took her out for dinner to celebrate their wrecked wedding day at the Mandarin Hotel. It was all over for her in her heart. Every girl dreamed of her wedding day, and hers was a total disaster and tragedy for her and her family.

Return to London to Resume Life and Higher Studies

Surendran and she were married legally, but the magic of their relationship was killed. Somewhere deep within, she had lost trust. They continued to love each other for four years before the coffin was nailed. Shreiyaa came out the more successful of the two, passing her law exams with flying colours and topping the faculty in the law of evidence, but Surendran never made it in law.

The Ceremonial Wedding

The wedding was held in a Hindu temple with their families still fighting and hostile. They decided to have the wedding, sanctified before God, at a Hindu temple. It was the last bid to save this marriage, but God did not bless it. They were preparing for the ceremonial wedding, and it was traditional for the groom's family to gift the bride with a new silk sari.

Mrs Chandran gave her an old sari from her wardrobe and said, 'What is the big deal? The next time she wears it is when she is dead.' It was obvious she hated Shreiyaa to the core. When Nandini heard of this, she said to Shreiyaa, 'You are making a big mistake getting married, but don't make the mistake of having children.' Those words went deep into Shreiyaa, and she made sure that they never had children. They were incompatible, their stars were incompatible, and what the astrologers had predicted was becoming more and more evident.

Surendran let life go without taking responsibility for his studies or his marriage. Shreiyaa urged him to come up in life so that they could make a life without parental interference, but he did not make any effort. They went through a ceremonial marriage, and on that day, as Shreiyaa was bringing a lit lamp into her in-laws' house (customary as a symbol of the goddess of wealth entering the household), Mrs Chandran stood in the garden of their palatial home and shouted in front of the wedding guests, 'I do not want this girl!'

Shreiyaa was supposed to have her feet washed by her mother-in-law before stepping into the house, but Mrs Chandran refused to. She embarrassed Shreiyaa's family and her in front of the wedding guests. Shreiyaa stayed for two weeks in the house after the wedding, but Mr and Mrs Chandran insulted her parents. She told Surendran, 'I fought with my parents to marry you, but I will not tolerate any insults against my parents.' Mr and Mrs Chandran would conjure up stories about her and make Surendran suspicious of her so that when she looked him in his eyes, they did not show love and tenderness anymore. They showed hostility and animosity. It would cause her and Surendran to get into heated arguments, and when she came out of the bedroom one evening when the couple were arguing, the in-laws had put their ears to the wall to eavesdrop as they wanted their son to fall out of love with her. Their love had been killed by his parents.

Honeymoon in Russia

Nevertheless, Surendran took her to Russia for their honeymoon but there was no more passion and love. The Kremlin was breath-taking and the Tzar's Palace where they dined had beautiful paintings in a multitude of colours on the ceilings. One of the most memorable romantic evenings they had was eating an Uzbekistan dinner in

Russia at the Tzar's palace. The food was just superb and they ended up eating a whole bunch of very large fresh juicy green grapes for dessert. They were so sweet and succulent and the colour was a lovely pale green. It was in Russia that Shreiyaa's Thali or Mangal Sutra broke, a very bad omen. She knew now that the predictions of the ancient wisdom and science of astrology were accurate and the astrologers were right.

Significance of the *Mangalsutra* in Hindu Marriages

This is a chain which could be made of black beads or a gold chain with an auspicious pendant with a motif of a god or goddess. It is put on the bride by the groom and signifies eternal love and the marriage bond. 'It is by this *mangalsutra* that I wed thee,' the groom says to his bride. It is also known as a *Thali*. It is a very holy chain, and it respects the sacrosanct institution of marriage and, in effect, means 'I will honour, respect, and love you for better or for worse till death do us part.' Only if the husband dies can the wife remove her mangalsutra, and in fact, she is expected to do so then. If you get divorced, it is the end of the marriage, and the mangalsutra loses its significance.

When they returned to London, their cat Princess also left them. It is an age-old superstition that when your cat leaves you, bad news is on the way. That too was a bad omen. Shreiyaa left Surendran in the year she was doing the English bar exams, as she knew that if she stayed in this marriage, his parents would wreck her and her spirit. They still loved each other, and it was the most painful ordeal for both of them. Surendran had not made it with his studies in England, and they had no choice but to stay with his parents and family.

Shreiyaa knew her life was in danger, and she was pre-empting a further tragedy, so she filed for divorce and nailed the coffin of their ill-fated love. When their divorce papers came through, Surendran and Shreiyaa held each other in a deep embrace and wept inconsolably; it was so sad, as the marriage had failed due to external interference. However, the lamp of their love was still burning in their hearts and soul. They had to move on and part ways, and it was stinging within him and her for years after the divorce. Their love lingered on even after the end of their marriage. Till today, there is a special place in her heart for Surendran even though he has remarried. They dated each other for fourteen years after the divorce and kept each other company to make the blow easier to handle and to cushion their sorrows and lick their wounds together. It was a fairy-tale love that ended tragically, and there was pain in her for a long time and for him too. It was all very unfair.

Towards the end of the fourth year of their marriage, it was becoming evident to both of them that they would part. When Shreiyaa returned after summer holidays in Singapore, Surendran opened an expensive bottle of champagne at Heathrow Airport, London, to welcome her back. When they came home, he had written love notes and poems in dedication to her in every room of their apartment in Highgate, and as she walked into every room, there was a huge bouquet of summer flowers with fresh fragrance that exuded in all the rooms. It was so romantic and idyllic, but the marriage was already on the rocks.

Their Last Christmas Together in England

On their last Christmas together, he cooked her a splendid roast goose. He also made an awesome pie using the recipe from the seventeenth-century royal kitchen of King Henry Frederick. He deboned a turkey, a chicken, and a duck and stuffed one into the other and also stuffed it with sausage and spinach. He then put an outer coating of short-crust pastry and baked it for hours. The end product was incredible. It had layers of colours, starting with golden pastry then poultry meat, pink sausage, and green spinach. The taste was indescribably good. They also had a Christmas cake that had been soaked in brandy for a year to celebrate the love they once had.

The saddest day in both their lives was the day their divorce papers arrived. They came together for a reason and a season but not for a lifetime as they had hoped and planned. Destiny had other plans for them, and destiny appeared very unkind.

Fate was unkind. Shreiyaa believes that if you don't get the blessings of your parents, nothing will ever go right. They moved on with the residue of love in their hearts and in pain and deep anguish.

Chapter 5

The Deep Abyss of Misery: Diagnosed with Bipolar Disorder

Shreiyaa's life after the divorce was a painful road to recovery. With this severe emotional upheaval and shock to her system, she had a complete nervous breakdown after graduating as barrister from the Bar of England and Wales. Surendran felt guilty and kept in constant touch with her.

Kishen, Nandini, and Hemanth were heartbroken too and aghast at what had happened. She was deeply depressed and suffered from amnesia for a brief period. Now they were divorced and separated back in Singapore. He tried hard to mend the broken pieces in Shreiyaa, feeling sad and sorry for her plight. She was too young to have her dreams broken to pieces. Surendran had also made propositions for them to reunite, but it was all over for her. She still loved him, but her trust had been betrayed—not by Surendran, but at the wickedness of his parents and family towards her and her family. The beautiful vase of fragrant flowers had shattered, and the flowers had withered and were dying; it could not be put back together again. That was the story of true love between Surendran and Shreiyaa. She was just twenty-five years old at that time, and she never for a moment blamed him, as her heart was still throbbing with love for him.

Surendran was truly helpless as he watched his loved one struggle and grapple with her painful issues. She was diagnosed with bipolar disorder, and Kishen and Nandini got the best doctors from the prestigious Mount Elizabeth Hospital to attend to her and put her back together. After qualifying as an English barrister with an upper second-class honours degree, she experienced a brief period where she had forgotten how to read and write English. She felt sensations of electric currents coming down from her head to her spine. Every time she tried to write, the words would appear zigzag on the paper. Four leading doctors battled to bring her back, and she was heavily sedated for two years.

A day in her life during the darkest moments was just sipping orange juice, eating, taking medicine, and falling into a deep sleep for hours on end. Nandini, in her desperation, consulted astrologers about her plight, and they promised that this was a temporary phase. They said she had her one wing cut off and was deeply wounded but one day the wing would grow back and she would fly high again.

Her parents had to make her wrap up boxes to rebuild her ability to concentrate and focus. She would cower back like a weak child and get exhausted after wrapping fifty a day. Kishen, Nandini, and Hemanth as a family were united in their resolve to bring her back and see to her healing and recovery. Eventually, they put her on a computer, and she started writing simple things. Slowly and surely, she was moving toward recovery.

Her Faith in Lord Krishna Shattered

All her dreams and her spirit had broken, and it broke her mind too. She rejected God and spent a lot of time in darkness, not believing in God. She was on medication, but her negativity towards God was an obstacle to her recovery and healing. She felt she could not step into another temple again. She could not understand why God was so cold and cruel to her and had designed such a painful fate. Kishen and Nandini kept praying for their daughter, and finally a Christian friend and missionary from Campus Crusade offered to take her on and pray for her.

She got involved with born-again Christians and rebuilt her faith in Jesus. Kishen was a little hurt, being a traditional Hindu, but Nandini encouraged it. Flora Ladder, who was this missionary, together with another strong Christian missionary, Audrey Bowet, prayed with her. This was an initial turning point, and her mind came back to her. Meanwhile, Surendran and Shreiyaa were still dating intermittently. He was full of the milk of human kindness and compassion and was deeply honourable on his dates. He was a friend and comforter that she could lean on, and there was never a physical connection. It made things easier to pull her back together again. Prayer sessions with the Christians saw a great improvement for her, and soon her amnesia was over. She started practising law and then went on Australia, Melbourne, for higher studies. She succeeded and obtained a LLM master's degree in law. She still kept in touch with Surendran, and their friendship was still deep, caring, and beautiful.

Fourteen Years Later

Fourteen years later, Surendran decided to remarry. By this time, Shreiyaa had grown up, and her wings had come back to her. She had made great strides in her life through her prayers and made new friends who supported her. She was deeply hurt when he broke the news to her. But years had gone by, and she decided to bless him with a good future. They met and talked about it, and he apologized abjectly for his shortcomings as a husband. And because it was true love, she found it in her heart to forgive him. Tears welled up in her eyes, but he did not see them; she wept in silence. It was time to let go, and there was no point in the separated, divorced couple staying in the 'Black Hole of Calcutta' any longer. Both of them had to move on, but the residue of love was still alive.

Surendran remarried, but after two years, she found her first birthday cards were still coming from him. It was obvious he still had her in his mind and in his heart. They resumed their friendship and met and talked on evening dinner dates, something which his current wife was in the dark about. Surendran's remarriage was an arranged one, and in Shreiyaa's heart, she was sure that the magic of the love they once shared was irreplaceable even if another woman took her place. The love they shared was special and could not be repeated with another woman.

Time went on, and one day she told Surendran, 'This is becoming ludicrous. I am now the other woman, and it is simply not right.' She wept at that point and asked Surendran to remind her why they had parted as she could not remember. He replied, 'There is no point thinking about it. I am now married for ten years, and girl, you have done so well. I have been watching you on the Internet. Move on. If you had not left you would not be who you are today.'

If it was any consolation, she knew in her heart that Surendran still admired her. In September 2010, they agreed to part and never see each other again. Even though their marriage only lasted four years, the relationship between them lasted a good thirty years.

Somewhere deep in her heart, the light of love burns for Surendran, and no one can stop that, not even his family or his current wife. Feelings are not something you can control. Circumstances were against them. But time heals, and the couple—no longer a couple—has moved on. Shreiyaa wishes Surendran the very best and wants him only to be happy. She would never come in the way of his new life, and it is the same for Surendran.

Many Suitors, Many Marriage Proposals

Shreiyaa's path after the divorce was strewn with many suitors and marriage proposals. Each suitor has to date met with a rejection from her. Her psyche on marriage has been damaged or tarnished, and she does not think this is the right option for her currently unless a miracle happens in the future. She has found love in so many others, like her friends, relatives, the chirping of birds, the morning dew, the mewing of cats, and the barking of dogs. The air that she breathes is fresh and fragrant once again. She has now no bitterness in her heart.

Beatrice and Andrea Giving Shreiyaa New Dreams

Her friends Beatrice and Andrea got together and paved the way for the morning glory to blossom in her life. They told her to write her first book and get it published and they would stand by her and help her. Andrea did all the editing of her first book and set her on the path to writing. This was the golden key in her life to a new destiny. It was from then on that she started writing. Beatrice's boyfriend was a tycoon, a billionaire, and when he heard her story, he decided to give her a break in life. During that one year that she worked for Tan Sri Amar Ali, a Malaysian tycoon, she experienced a treasure trove of fairy-tale travelling experiences.

Jet-Setting

She was jet-setting on private jets and first-class flights around Europe, travelling like never before. She had breakfast in Egypt, lunch in Düsseldorf, and dinner in Paris. Tan Sri was so kind to her, just like Beatrice, and they even gave her shopping money in Egypt to spend at the souk.

Egyptian Souk

The souks, or the local markets, and the larger bazaars are amongst the most remarkable attractions of Egypt. Unlike Lebanon, Syria, and Turkey, Egypt doesn't really have a restaurant culture although it does have an exciting street food scene. Located behind and around the Temple of Luxor, Sharia el-Souq was converted into a charming yet unauthentic covered pedestrian zone. The newly paved and renovated street accommodates many shops that sell that same Egyptian merchandise, catering to tourists. While items are the same, the pleasant surroundings make for a generally better shopping experience, albeit highly artificial.

Aswan Souk is located about four blocks from the River Nile. It is an open-air bazaar with the most exquisite and exotic items of the Middle East sold here. It is colourful with carpets and tapestries with Egyptian designs on them. There are also plenty of Egyptian and African goods and a wide variety of dried hibiscus flowers, perfumes, nuts, henna powder, and ancient Egyptian souvenirs. There are also T-shirts, spices, and cheap saffron—probably the cheapest you can get anywhere. (The saffron, however, cannot be compared in quality with the varieties from Spain.) This souk is also known locally as Sharia As Souq. It winds down to many alleyways, and in every nook and corner, you can find Egyptian salesmen calling out to you to see their goods, hoping they would make their sale for the day.

Dinner on the River Nile and Belly Dancing

A dinner cruise on the Nile River at night with a belly show is one of the most interesting activities you can have at night in Cairo. They enjoyed sailing with a delicious Egyptian meze dinner and an Egyptian folklore show and a belly dancer. *Meze* is the Egyptian version of tapas, a collection of small dishes that can be enjoyed individually as appetizers or together as a meal. There were about eight choices each of hot and cold dishes, and they were able to choose which ones they wanted to sample. They thoroughly enjoyed the evening out on the Nile River in Cairo.

Horse Riding in the Desert of Giza near the Pyramids

In the hot, scorching sun of the deserts of Giza, they went horse riding up to the pyramids. One of the seven ancient wonders of the world, the great pyramids of Giza, are marvellous feats of architecture.

The Giza complex consists of three large pyramids built for the pharaohs Khufu, Khafre, and Menkaure.

The grand structures were built between 2589 BC and 2504 BC. How they were built has been a source of debate. The pyramids are part of the Giza necropolis that also houses the Great Sphinx, smaller pyramids for queens, and several complexes for the workers. Historians agree there was an immense amount of labour involved; the technical ingenuity and skill that went into the pyramids help the structures remain standing today.

The Ritz in Paris

On these global-trotting expeditions with Beatrice and Tan Sri Amar Ali, Shreiyaa stayed at the Ritz Paris. The decor was like seventeenth-century interior design, so opulent. These were God's compensations to her.

The Hotel Ritz is located in central Paris and is ranked amongst one of the most luxurious hotels in the world. The service provided in this hotel is simply impeccable, with professional waiters and waitress waiting on you hand and foot and greeting you with a warm smile. It hosts major and world-renowned dignitaries, film stars, and musicians. The interior decor is par excellence with spotlights all over the rooms. The fridge is filled with goodies, and there is a bar counter which offers vintage wine and champagne like Dom Pérignon.

She has also heard that it offers an exorbitant beluga caviar facial, which is the height of indulgence. It is a hotel which offers the zenith of luxury. It seems that the Imperial, the grandest suite of the hotel, is listed by the French government as a national monument. Suites are named after luminaries such as Coco Chanel and Ernest Hemingway, who stayed there over some time. Some of the most sought-after chefs work in this hotel and cook the most expensive and high-end meals for the rich and famous.

For Shreiyaa, it was something she never in her remotest dreams ever thought she would experience, and while she stayed there, she wondered what she had ever done to deserve this.

Staying at the Crown Melbourne

One of the trips was to Melbourne, and she was on first class in Singapore Airlines, eating beluga caviar all the way to Melbourne. Shreiyaa stayed at a seven-star hotel and had the time of her life.

Crown Melbourne is a seven-star hotel with its own casino and an entertainment complex. It is situated on the Southbank of the Yarra River. This was yet another magnificent experience of indulgence and the high life for her. Nearby are lots of shops that sell high-end products and lots of restaurants. She was given US$1,000 to gamble with at the casino but did not do so, because she does not believe in gambling. To her, the US$1,000 was already a windfall. While she was enjoying all these luxurious tours in her job with Tan Sri Amar Ali, her heart was still thinking of the underprivileged, who could never even breathe a dream like this. Some people in this world didn't get enough to eat, so to her, though she enjoyed it, she thought to herself this was sinful wastage of money!

First Book Published

Shreiyaa discovered a gift for writing, which was brought out by the joint efforts of Beatrice and Andrea. It was an eventful book launch and the discovery of a new self-worth, a new dream, and a new motivation in life. It tilled the soil for many more books to come and many articles to be published. She made it to the press on this book, and many people congratulated her.

Chapter 6

Turning Point

This happened when a friend, Jolene introduced her to Buddhism, which she embraced wholeheartedly. She found it closer to her family's Hindu beliefs, and she started praying diligently every day. In her heart, she believed there was one god and all religions led to the one same god. Though Buddhism did not believe in God, she believed in God and in the principles of Buddhism. This helped her fully recover from her ordeal and embark on a new journey into spirituality, a great antidote to her injured feelings.

Audience with His Holiness the Dalai Lama

In 2006 she had an audience with His Holiness the Dalai Lama, and it turned her life around. His teachings blessed her life.

Who Is the Dalai Lama?

Tenzin Gyatso, His Holiness, the fourteenth Dalai Lama of Tibet, was born on 6 July 1935 in a small farming village of Taktser in the province of Amdo, north-east Tibet.

It is true that he sincerely believes that there is nothing extraordinary about himself, but the world at large or at least a significant part of it thinks otherwise.

A bright star shines in the midst of the chaos of this world, and no matter how genuine his self-effacement, the Dalai Lama is no ordinary monk. Precious gems of divine wisdom and heavenly compassion flow like a river from the heart of His Holiness and spread across the globe, cutting across oceans, continents, and mountains to bring peace and joy to the despondent and desolate. A fountain of fresh hope stems from the very core of his heart, bringing comfort to the wounded soul and answers to the earnest seeker of truth and love from north, south, east, and west of the globe.

Ordinary monks do not get recognized as the world's conscience keeper; neither do they win the Nobel Prize. And they don't get courted by heads of state, celebrities, movie stars, and scientists with equal exuberance and respect. The Dalai Lama, that most human of human beings, is a touch of divine grace that has inspired people from all walks of life all over the world to fall at his feet in reverence, yet he is the very epitome of humility.

At the tender age of two, he was chosen, recognized, and shortlisted as the reincarnation of his predecessor, the thirteenth Dalai Lama, and there the world found a spiritual leader who has made historical and phenomenal landmarks and continues to edify mankind. He was brought to the capital, Lhasa, in October 1939 and formally installed as the head of state of Tibet on February 22, 1940.

The newly established communist China invaded Tibet in 1949. Despite tireless efforts on the part of the Dalai Lama to bring about a peaceful resolution, the Chinese responded violently, destroying the very essence of the Tibetan culture and spiritual heritage. The roof the world, perhaps the holiest land of the East, was beset with doom and havoc as the Chinese continued their atrocities, creating disillusionment and resentment amongst the Tibetans, who aired their sentiment by staging armed uprisings which erupted in Lhasa on 10 March 1959. His Holiness was advised to flee the country, and on 17 March 1959, he crossed safely into India, where he was warmly received and given asylum.

Approximately eighty thousand Tibetan refugees followed His Holiness into exile and are now resettled primarily in India, Nepal, Bhutan, Switzerland, the United States, and Canada. His Holiness, in his plight to save his people and the Tibetan culture, began a peaceful struggle to preserve Tibet's unique identity and regain the country's independence. The culmination of this struggle saw the award of the Nobel Peace Prize on 10 December 1989 to His Holiness. The Nobel Committee emphasized 'that the Dalai Lama, in his struggle for the liberation of Tibet, consistently has opposed the use of violence. He has instead advocated peaceful solutions based upon tolerance and mutual respect in order to preserve the historical and cultural heritage of his people.'

McLeod Ganj, Dharamshala, the Official Residence of His Holiness

McLeod Ganj is named after a lieutenant governor of Punjab, David McLeod, and Forsyth Ganj is named after a divisional commissioner. Dharamshala is situated in the northern Indian state of Himachal Pradesh. Mountains dominate the scenery of McLeod Ganj. They form a treacherous range that creates unpredictable weather, passes 2,400 metres (8,900 feet), and provides a route for the herdsmen of the Ravi Valley beyond. A breathtaking snow-capped range will greet your eyes. McLeod Ganj is nine kilometres by bus and four kilometres by taxi from Kotwali Bazaar. While inhabitants of lower Dharamshala are almost all Indians, McLeod Ganj is primarily a Tibetan area. McLeod Ganj is surrounded by pine, Himalayan oak, rhododendron, and deodar forests. The main crops grown by local Indians in the valley below McLeod Ganj are rice, wheat, and tea.

Shreiyaa's Journey

Up in the mountains of Dharamshala, Shreiyaa braved hairpin bends and winding narrow roads with breathtaking snow-capped ranges to receive the blessing of His Holiness. When Shreiyaa arrived in Dharamshala with her uncle from the Indian diplomatic service and his family, she was told that her audience that was arranged months earlier with Tenzin Geyche, the former PA of HH Dalai Lama and former prime minister of the Tibetan government in exile, was cancelled. They said His Holiness was under the weather.

Shreiyaa said, 'No, His Holiness will see me.' She was ill, and she felt like the lady from Samaria in the Bible, who knew and said about Jesus, 'If I could just touch his robe, I would heal.' Within five minutes, His Holiness gave the word that he would see Shreiyaa. Her uncle told her it was his diplomatic connections, but she insisted that it was her strong faith and that His Holiness heard her inner call and plea from her heart for help. He came to her, as she was the only one at the audience that got a medicine Buddha from the divine hands of His Holiness. She wept in joy, as it was a telepathic connection between His Holiness and herself.

His Holiness is her guru, and in her deepest of sorrows and darkest hours, she still can connect with him from Singapore. His protective hand is always on her, and she surmount hurdles and challenges with his compassionate hand on her as he protects her from dangers.

He is the living Avalokiteshvara for all Buddhists, which is the god or goddess of compassion. The god or goddess of compassion in Tibetan Buddhism or Vajrayana Buddhism is Tara, and in Mahayana Buddhist, it is Kwan Imm. The story goes that Lord Buddha looked down on the earth and saw people praying and getting what they did not ask for and not getting what they asked for. So he shed a teardrop from heaven, and from that teardrop, the goddess of compassion blossomed from a splendid pink lotus. His Holiness is Tara or Kwan Imm.

Shreiyaa cries whenever she connects with His Holiness; it is an awesome, divine experience.

That Shreiyaa was blessed was no other than the will of the Almighty. Her heart beat fast in excitement as she looked on the kindly face of

His Holiness, who gently took hold of her hand and gave her a Buddha. The experience was awesome and blissful; a strange sense of calmness and peace enveloped her as she reached out to receive His Holiness's divine grace.

She will cherish this day, 16 April 2006, till her dying day as she knows she touched the hand of a living god.

His Holiness the Dalai Lama Transforms Shreiyaa's Life

Kishen and Nandini had planted the seeds of doing noble works for the community to both Hemanth and Shreiyaa; however, after the audience with His Holiness the Dalai Lama, these holistic principles became even more embedded in her outlook and lifestyle. Helping people less fortunate than her helped her to heal because she did not focus on her pain and suffering. She read widely on the austerities His Holiness had to face on the issue of Tibet in *My land and My People* and *Freedom in Exile*, and it gave her inspiration to follow his cardinal principles of adopting a life of non-violence. It has given her a purpose in life and given her deep, inner cleansing instead of carrying the cross of injured feelings from her marriage that failed.

Shreiyaa got heavily involved with doing noble deeds and charity work. She served the disabled at the Singapore Red Cross Society and gave much of her savings to the poor beggars in India whenever she visited India on spiritual retreats, which she did very often. When she went to Bangkok on a stint of work, she helped many beggars on the streets distributing money and buns to them. She also fed lots of hungry stray dogs and cats on the streets of Bangkok.

Today, she works as a writer and is also deeply involved in her spiritual pursuits of doing wholesome charity work. She teaches orphans and children from dysfunctional families as a volunteer at the Ramakrishna Mission Singapore. She is guided by the chief reverend of Singapore Buddhist Mission and has a spiritually rewarding relationship with him and also the Hindu swamis or priests of Ramakrishna Mission Singapore. She is also close to the Mother Teresa Nuns of Missionaries of Charities. She has one God and many masters who guide her. It is her faith that had brought her through, and it is growing day by day. She has lots of friends and is very stable and deeply spiritual. Though she lost the love of her life, she has found love in the greater community and believes in doing good for the greater good of all.

She has also won an award for her writing from a local newspaper. Today she has authored, co-authored, and ghost-written sixteen books, and five of her publications are in thirty-one worldwide library holdings. She also made it to the press on two occasions for her publications. Two of her books are well received by the United Nations in Geneva, and she is on a new journey as an author and has met new people and gone to many new places and is on the threshold of more blessings to come.

Shreiyaa's Message

I took to writing, but others may have other gifts from God. Cultivate good hobbies and interests, like baking, cooking, painting, or exercising by doing power walks and feeling the breeze of mother nature on your skin. Mother Nature is a great healer, and as you walk along the beach, the sea breeze will clear your toxins and bruised emotions. Cooking and baking for your friends as guinea pigs will soon earn you lots of compliments, and this will enhance your confidence and allow you to stand on your own two feet. The universe will bless you with a good support system of good and sincere friends, and thereby you will heal.

Master your hobbies. Be the best sculptor or artist you can be, and soon your products will be items for sale and appreciated by others. You can become well renowned for the skill you cultivated and has become a master of. Soon you will carve a niche for yourself, and this interest will bring you to greater heights and bring you to new and meaningful relationships and to new places too.

In my case, my writing took me around the world, and I met so many lovely people that it gave me a motivation to live my life and make the most and best out of it. You will find new avenues of inspiration, and you will have new aspirations and new dreams, which you can rebuild on, and the blessings will just flow into your life from the Master Provider. He will never abandon you even in the darkest moment. He will hold your hand and bring you out of your sorrows and bring new light into your life. That is the greatness of GOD ALMIGHTY. Whatever His will, let His will be done, as we are but mud and He is the master sculptor who will build you again no matter how broken you are.

Everyone gets a second chance and many, many chances in life. Sometimes He will send people to forewarn you of imminent dangers or to steer your course in a different direction. Be humble enough to accept these as messages from the holy, divine masters, as God speaks to us through our parents' wisdom, our family and friends too. Don't be afraid to be alone, as it is in times of loneliness that you are open to the greatest and richest messages from God. You may call it intuition, but they are from the holy Master, so be subservient enough to accept the divine guidance, and you will find yourself always protected.

For the people who came in and out of my life, each one made an indelible impression, and I hold the memories close to me for those who showed me love because to me love is the most precious commodity. That is what you remember most of people. People walk in and out of our lives, but only angels leave footprints in your heart. Life is a journey. Make it a beautiful journey, and give love everywhere. Love will come back to you, and you don't have to be married to experience love; it is with everyone. My heart is full of love, and I have lots of love in my life because God sends angels to me and because I bow down to my God every single day. He sends me loving people, and it is such pure love—the love of God.

In life, be ever ready to say thank you or sorry if you should say so, and be grateful for every blessing, which you should count every day. Humility and gratitude are virtues worth cultivating. Remember, there no is such thing as independence; we are all dependent on each other. You should build your relationships with others, and when you build others, God will build you too. Make God your central focus. As the Bible says, 'Seek ye first the kingdom and all its righteousness and then all other thing will be added on to you.' This means your house, your finances, your car, your soulmate, your lottery win will be added on to you, but your motivation should be to love God unconditionally. Even if the lottery win does not come, there will be other treasures at the end of the rainbow.

In Buddhism, it is said, 'First have good morals then have good friends and live in a good environment. Then you will secure a good life.' Whatever religion or faith you come from, make God the first love in your life. All other blessings will come from the master provider. Let go of the bad past, as there is new future for you. Maybe things went wrong because there were lessons to learn from the bad past. God is a forgiving god and a boundlessly compassionate one. If you change your negativity to positivity, He will bless you in the way He wants to.

Remember to say every day when you make your petitions and pleas to God, 'Thy will be done, Lord.' It is not 'My will be done' because in life you should surrender your life to God and let him bless you. You need to deserve the blessing, so on the way, you may be tested. So do your best to learn lessons from your failures, as failure is a stepping stone to success.

As for me, I am praying too that I will make it and live a holy life to deserve blessings and pass God's test of my character. He will also help you to pass the test; that is how great GOD's compassion is. His mercies are boundless. This is a great god, you know, a very great god. Live in His glory and worship Him every single day of your life because He is worthy of praise and worship. God is not asking for too much. He is only asking us to live a holy, clean life and have character and good principles. He will reward you, and I trust my God that my destiny ahead is in His hands. Glorify and honour God's name always, and in return, He will glorify and honour your life and destiny.

Love one another as God has loved you, and if you have misunderstandings with people that ends up in altercations, don't continue the altercation. Just walk away because new loving people will enter your life, and you can build new meaningful relationships. Life is dynamic. There is a new movie every day in your life, so live, experience, and enjoy it. It is magical, and life is beautiful despite the ups and downs. It is in your dark hours when you learn your biggest lessons, and when you have learnt it, you become wiser. You should apply that wisdom to your life.

I believe that saying thank you and sorry can melt the hearts of people around you, so be ready to use these words all the time in your life. He is a god of second, third chances, and in fact umpteen chances. To me, there is only one God Almighty, the one true beloved, and you must love Him unconditionally in good times and in bad. We must have religious tolerance and love one another. We take different paths, like different rivers converging into the big ocean of divinity, from where all blessings flow.

I am proud to be Singaporean, as my country is multireligious, multiracial, and multicultural, and we live in harmony with their diverse cultures. This is what my country taught me—to care for everyone and respect the views of others. If you have difference of opinions on religious matters or cultural matters, don't make an issue of it—just agree to disagree. If you get into a negative relationship with someone, don't make it worse by trying to prove your point and asserting that you are right; just walk away from it.

In Buddhism, they say we should avoid the five poisons of disturbing emotions, which are desire, anger, delusion or ignorance, pride, and jealousy. Do not curse others, as the negativity will only boomerang back into your life. As the Christians say, bless your enemies and overcome evil with good. Don't just be a good citizen of your country; be a good citizen of the world. This way, you can cultivate world peace, and that is what we want—a world with no wars, a world that is beautiful to live in so we can all find paradise on earth. In your prayer requests, don't just ask for blessings for yourself alone; learn to pray and bless others too.

Remember, the most important thing and the best gift you can give those you love and care for is the gift of faith. Praying for them is more noble than any other gift in life. Be gentle as a lamb when handling others; you will make lots of meaningful, lasting relationships along the way. Spread love and good will everywhere you go. And remember most of all, God is love!

Shreiyaa's Message to Divorcing Couples

I have a message for divorcing couples. If circumstances are bad in your marriage and you can't work at it any more, then as a compassionate couple, you need to work out your divorce and handle each other gently. You need to be friends and not be hostile and have animosity for each other, as you both are wounded souls. You need to cushion the blow and nurture each other. After all, at one point in time, you knew and shared the bed of love and lovemaking together, which is a deep emotional and spiritual union. You can't run away from your ex-spouse, as you have soul ties that need to be cut with gentleness and kindness, just like the umbilical cord of a newborn babe has to be severed from his or her mother.

Husband and wife are one in flesh and spirit when they are wed, and you should take time to nurture each other out to the road of independence. If your marriage did not work out, it is probably an act of God or fate that you can't live together any more, and you must help pull each other together again so that you both can move on in life with no more ties and negative emotions of anger, hatred, and bitterness in your heart. It makes it much easier for divorcing couples, but you can only do this if you are mature enough and you are humane enough to understand that giving a helping hand to your ex-spouse is a natural way for you to heal too.

I am proud to say that Surendran and I did this for each other, and our soul ties were eventually severed with finesse and decorum.

When you have no bitterness in your heart and you are able to forgive others for the pain and emotional injuries they have caused you, you are on your way to healing. You are on your way to recovery, and the floodgates of heaven will bless you and your new journey in life. Heaven will have in front of you a new plan and a fresh blessing. No matter what the injury and hard as it may be, don't wish the party who hurt you any ill. This takes courage and faith in GOD ALMIGHTY. Destiny may have other great plans in your life, and you can end doom and gloom and bloom again.

Let go in love, and you will find love again. It may not be in one person, but you will find it in humanity, in nature, in the chirping of birds, in the laughter of a child, or in the grin of an old person that you lent a helping hand to. Read motivational books. Listen to uplifting music, and pray. Meditate and fill your life with good deeds and have good morals. Be humble in life, as you are no one unless God makes something out of you. We are all but an instrument of his will, and there is no point carrying pain, anger, and anguish for too long, as the only one that gets hurt is you alone. There is a big world out there. Go out and make it again.

Sometimes people hurt you because they have a wrong perception of you and they judge you by that perception. And you just may not be the wrongdoer, but that is life. Don't be angry and don't be bitter and don't be vengeful, as it will only bounce back to you. Do good and feel good again. Forgive your past, as your destiny ahead is the echo of your thoughts and how you feel. Do on to others what you would do on to yourself, and forgiveness will send a ripple into the universe that will harness great blessings for you.

Most of all learn to love yourself again. Don't jump into a new relationship when you have not healed, as it is, as the cliché goes, 'jumping from the fire into the frying pan'. If you are meant to marry again, you will know when you meet the next prospective partner whether he or she is compassionate enough to take you with your past. If not, single living is fine too. There is freedom and, as the old adage goes, 'it is better to have loved and lost than never to have loved at all'.

Prayers are a great tonic to take away the toxins of bruised emotions, and you should immerse yourself in deep prayer and navigate your life to better things once again. The road may be painful, but there will be light at the end of the dark tunnel if you lean on God for strength. This is the road less travelled, but it is a wholesome one where you will see good, positive results. You can carve a new destiny and a good one. Don't carry baggage; instead carry a bag of good deeds, and open the door of your heart to love again and love one and all. The key to opening the door of your heart again is to let go of bad experiences and forgive even if you can't forget. You can do all this only if your spiritual life is strong and you are deeply anchored in your faith. You will naturally find the inner strength that God will give you.

Thirty-One Years after the Marriage Broke Down

Thirty-one years later, Surendran's mother was now in her ripe, old age. She asked to see Shreiyaa. Still a little wounded, Shreiyaa wanted to keep her self-respect and provide a stage of high emotions. She sent one of her masterpieces—a book—to Surendran, wishing him the very best in life. She wrote a note to Surendran and told him that if his second marriage worked out, it was not because he got a better wife but because he just got a wife the family treated better!

In fact, earlier on, Shreiyaa was accused by Mrs Chandran of marrying Surendran for the wealth of the Chandran family. So at the time of divorce in London, when the lawyers told her she was entitled to maintenance, she decided to forgo her legal rights, as her self-respect and her principles were more important to her. She had married for love, and there was no scheming agenda in her, as she was a very young woman when she fell in love and had to pay painfully for just falling in love.

Aside from that, she came from a respectable family of means and status in society. In a private conversation with Surendran, he admitted to her that their marriage was wrecked by his mother, and that was a major source of consolation to her, as he knew and endorsed the fact that Shreiyaa was an honest woman. That was very important to her. She owed all her answers and how she lived her life to the one beloved God Almighty.

Years later, all was forgiven, and she had moved on. Shreiyaa wished Mrs Chandran peace and good health. Shreiyaa believes that if you are able to forgive the person who hurt you the most in life, the battle is all over, and you come out a winner standing on very high ground. This sort of strength comes only from deep prayer, as it is God who helps you to come to terms with the things you can't change and helps you to forgive. Live and let live, and you begin to feel an inner cleansing. The feeling is just simply beautiful.

Shreiyaa admits, for many years, she harboured ill feeling, anger, resentment, deep pain of rejection, and dejection towards Mrs Chandran. But she decided not to take it to her grave, nor should she let Mrs Chandran take it to her grave. His Holiness the Dalai Lama told her to forgive, and she did. Shreiyaa believes that we are all stronger than we think and sometimes it takes a crisis to bring out that strength. A Buddhist scholar once said, 'You must leave this world a better place than you found it!' And that is what she wants to do!

Today

Kishen; Nandini; Hemanth; his wife, Sharmila; and their son, Nikhil, are all proud of her. Friends are proud of her, and today she can hold her head up high and stand on her own feet. Although she is on lifelong medication, she has an excellent doctor standing by her. He guides her and helps her surmount her hurdles and cope with her challenges. Her divine masters from Singapore Buddhist Mission and Ramakrishna Mission, together with her guru, His Holiness the Dalai Lama, are bottomless pits of compassion, and this is God's grace flowing from His divine throne. She also goes to the Catholic Church and attends masses to hear good sermons to elevate her mind with a view to cultivate lofty ideals. The rivers of crystal-clear waters run in her life to sustain and nourish her.

Faith can move mountains; never give up God for even a moment. God turned a calamity into a blessing. She lives each day in complete dependence on God, and He never lets her down. She is surrounded by love, and she lives for her beloved parents, family, and friends, who nurtured her through the darkest days of her life. Today there is a breaking of a new dawn with lots of sunshine.

Kishen and Nandini, in their old age, bought a house each for Hemanth and Shreiyaa and sorted out their inheritance during their lifetime. Kishen is now ninety-six years old, and Nandini is eighty-eight years old. They know and are peaceful that their children are well and happy despite the odds that Shreiyaa has had to face in her life.

Creating a New Destiny the Best I Could

Shreiyaa believes fate and destiny are two different concepts. Fate is the life you lead without putting yourself in the path of achieving greatness. If you move into a path in life without effort, that is your fate, and your fate could be bad or good. When your fate is bad, you can still create a good destiny ahead of you. You need to do inner cleansing. Find inner strength and courage to rise above your bad phase and path. Get out of your tragic situation, and aim for higher goals in life. You need to feel inspired to recreate and rewrite the chapters in your life.

Here is where you hang on to faith in God or faith in yourself, and always check your own inner being. Check your character, and be the nicest person you can be to others. You will find that when you put out goodness, goodness returns to you. Take away feelings of anger, revenge, resentment, and jealousy, and instead come out of any situation smelling like a rose with good, positive emotions. Remember, if you shoot feelings of revenge, resentment, jealousy, and anger, it will just come back to you. 'What goes around comes around', as the old adage goes. Meditation and prayer can invoke positive emotions in your dealings with others, and you can propel forward, creating a harmonious and good destiny. So if your fate is bad, remember that your destiny can still be good and you can recreate that. Don't stay in the muddied pool but strive to see the resplendent sunshine and blossom like a morning glory.

Shreiyaa had to take the step of faith and create her own destiny from the cruel fate of her failed marriage. As His Holiness says, 'Suffering is inevitable, but it is optional.' She opted not to suffer in a bad marriage. She decided to chase the rainbow and find the treasure at the end of it, and she reached for the stars in the sky and moved forward.

She chose her own destiny when fate was cruel to her, a destiny still in the making, but her choices led her to what she is today and where she is. Shreiyaa is now straight into the arms of the people who truly love and care for her. She picked up the pieces of her broken life along the way to pursue one of her lifelong dreams—of being a published author—and make it a reality. In the process, she found love everywhere. Shreiyaa believes you can create a wholesome destiny for yourself even if your fate was bad and rewrite the chapters of your life in any situation of tragedy and turn your life around.

> Destiny has two ways of crushing us—by refusing our wishes and by fulfilling them. (Henri Frederic Amiel)

A new life has begun, and the MORNING GLORY HAS BLOSSOMED!

Printed in the United States
By Bookmasters